Praise for *Ava*

"Through crisp, authoritative prose, Dillon's expertise and empathy shine, making this seemingly impossible genetic innovation feel eerily plausible in the novel's not-so-farfetched political and legislative landscape."—**BookLife Reviews, editor's pick**

"*Ava* is a stunning debut that confronts the inevitable intersection of science, motherhood, and bodily autonomy with unflinching honesty."—**Tanya Chernov, author of *A Real Emotional Girl***

"As an avid reader I always look for books that make a difference, that entertain and also educate. The lessons in *Ava* are relevant and important, and Victoria Dillon weaves these lessons throughout her book in a brilliant way. It is obvious Dillon has done her homework and the extensive research that makes this book possible. This is definitely a 5-star read."—**Laura L. Engel, author of *You'll Forget This Ever Happened***

AVA

a novel

VICTORIA DILLON

SHE WRITES PRESS

Published in 2026 by
She Writes Press, an imprint of The Stable Book Group

32 Court Street, Suite 2109
Brooklyn, NY 11201
https://shewritespress.com
Library of Congress Control Number: 2025919165
ISBN: 979-8-89636-086-5
eISBN: 979-8-89636-087-2

Interior Designer: Andrea Reider
Interior illustrations: Arun Kumar
Printed in the United States

To Graham McCormick.

You were the best of all the good eggs in this world.

PROLOGUE

Tap-tap-tap.

"Easy now . . . easy."

"Yes, yes. I know. I'm being easy."

Tap-tap.

"Can you see his hair? What color is it?"

Sigh.

Tap-tap-tap-tap-tap-tap.

"Still nothing?"

"Please, just let us focus, okay?"

Tap-tap-tap-tap.

CRACK.

Gasp.

"That's it! Peel off the rest of it!"

"So, is his hair brown?"

"Please, Mom . . . give us a sec, okay?"

Pieces of glistening shell drop to the floor, revealing remnants of amnion coating a head of thick, brown hair. Gently, after the rest of the shell is removed to expose his ruddy, smooth skin, the young couple dries off their new baby boy.

PART I

CHAPTER 1

September 3, 2031
AP News
Nashville mother of two dies "senselessly" from untreated ectopic pregnancy, pro-choice advocates assert

I can't breathe . . . I can't breathe . . .

Larkin coughed and wheezed as she fell to her hands and knees in the warm grass near the Rock, a well-known landmark at the edge of the University of Tennessee campus. Her eyes burned and watered as she tried to focus on the blurry figures rushing past her as they screamed in panic and yelled obscenities. She started to crawl in their direction, past the large hunk of dolomite that was now splattered with red paint, covering the orange-and-white checkerboard pattern that had been there that morning.

Someone grabbed her wrist and yanked her upright. She stumbled behind them, using her other hand to wipe her eyes with her shirt, her backpack rhythmically striking her back each time her feet hit the ground. The stranger yelled to her as they ran, but the surrounding chaos muffled their voice. Something covered the stranger's mouth and nose, and Larkin wished she had thought to bring a bandana. She tried to reply and at least say thank you, but she could only let out a raspy hack.

They hurried between two buildings and, after a brief sprint, abruptly stopped. Larkin could tell she was in a shaded area as the air felt cooler. The stranger guided her to a folding chair and helped her take off her backpack, reassuring her she would be okay before saying a quick goodbye.

Next, she heard a woman's voice, gravelly from age and too many cigarettes.

"I'm Maxine, Ms. Puffy Eyes. I'm a nurse, and I'm here to help you," she said with fatigued sympathy. "Hold your head back. Let's get this crap washed out of your eyes."

The cold saline was a welcome relief to Larkin's throbbing eyes. She held her head back as the liquid poured down her face and onto her T-shirt. Maxine stopped now and then for Larkin to sputter and cough.

"Did you lose your friends in this mess?" Maxine asked as Larkin caught her breath.

"No, I came alone after my shift at the bookstore. I wasn't here very long when all of this happened."

"Well, I've been helping at these protests for a long time," she said as she flushed Larkin's eyes once more. Holding Larkin's chin and moving her head from left to right, Maxine added, "Always the same old, same old. Something really pisses folks off, like that poor young lady in Nashville. They gather and make clever signs that might be seen on the news. They get petitions signed and write to their congressmen. And in a few days, things die down, and nothing changes until the next outrage, and it starts all over again, whether it's about gun control, abortion, or whatever, you know? Same thing. We haven't had a real win since '73, and it's been nothing but losses since then."

"So, do you think we are wasting our time? That *I'm* wasting my time?"

"Your heart's in the right place and your cause is good, but this isn't working, is it?" Maxine said as she stopped flushing

Larkin's eyes. She put her hand on her hip, waiting impatiently for a reply.

"No. It's really not," Larkin quietly agreed. "So, do you have any suggestions?"

"I'm seventy-nine, and I'm tired. I'm all out of suggestions," she said dryly. "But you all keep showing up, so I'll keep showing up to help you."

"I appreciate it."

"You don't have to thank me. Just promise me you'll think of some other way to fix this shit show, okay?"

Larkin nodded and dabbed her eyes with the back of her hand. She felt better, but the saline had washed out her contacts. Larkin squinted to focus, but Maxine was only a blurry visage.

"You should be good now. You can rest here a bit. I need to get on to the next well-intentioned idiot." She sighed and lumbered away.

"Alright, Mr. Raven Hair," Larkin heard Maxine say with the same lack of enthusiasm. "Looks like you're going to need some staples to that gash on your head."

Unable to drive without her contacts, Larkin had to walk the mile to her apartment. Once there, she put on her glasses and lay down on her couch. She sent a quick text to her parents, letting them know she was safe—they had sent increasingly urgent messages asking where she was. She scrolled through her social media accounts and saw the photos her friends had posted of protests at other universities and city centers. Most had ended the same way this one had: tear gas and disarray. Some of her friends had been hit with batons or rubber bullets. A few of them had been arrested and needed bail money. She sent them what she could through her cash app.

She closed her eyes and hoped that it would be different this time. That this time, change would come. But she knew Maxine was right.

CHAPTER 2

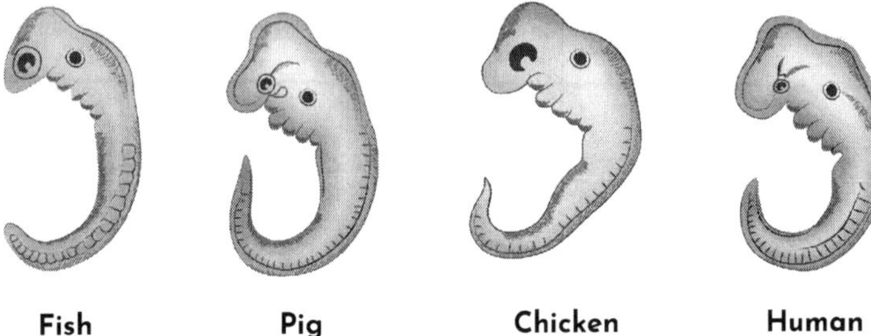

The soft tapping of computer keys provided a disciplined white noise. Larkin was studying alone in the library during her senior year of college, as she had most Sundays for the past three years. Her eyes were still a little swollen from the day before, but her cough was better. She checked her phone to see if her best friend, Aubrey, had replied to an earlier message, but it was still unread. Larkin supposed she was consumed with the premed classes she was taking at Vanderbilt, a few hours away, and went back to taking notes.

Another student joined her at the smooth-grained cherry table. He hung his backpack on his chair and sat catty-corner from Larkin, where he opened his laptop and placed a large calculator beside it. Muttering to himself, he looked at his phone with concern.

"Excuse me," he whispered. "Do you have a charger I can borrow? My battery is dying, and my phone's at 2 percent."

"I think so," Larkin replied as she dug through the front pocket of her well-worn backpack, which lay on the table. She rummaged past a pack of gum, hand sanitizer, and mint lip balm. When she felt a cord at the bottom, she handed it to him.

"Thank you so much." He sighed with relief. "Part of my class notes are on my phone. I would have been screwed without them."

Larkin smiled politely and went back to her reading, glancing up at her new tablemate now and then. Thick, wavy, jet-black hair spilled over his forehead in large curls. He had to brush them away often, revealing his sky-blue eyes. When he smiled, she noticed a small chip in his upper front tooth. She thought about asking him how he'd gotten the chip, but he was probably asked that all the time. Strangers often asked her how tall she was and if she played basketball. The answer was always "five feet, ten inches" and "no." She always felt self-conscious about her height being wasted when those strangers looked disappointed by her reply.

When he reached for a pencil he had dropped, his hair fell forward again, and she noticed the glint of stainless steel staples on the side of his head, embedded in dried, crusted blood.

"I'm Larkin, by the way."

"Larkin," he repeated, as if burning the name into his memory. "Nice to meet you. I'm Spencer."

"I think I know you as Mr. Raven Hair. I'm also known as Ms. Puffy Eyes to Nurse Maxine." She smiled.

"So that was you getting drenched in water?" Spencer chuckled. "I think we kept her pretty busy tending to all of us misguided morons. She gave me a pretty good lecture on wasting my time after I got whacked with a can of tear gas."

"I got the same lecture, and she does have a point."

Spencer nodded as he distractedly rubbed his wound. "Do you mind if I ask what you're studying?"

"I'm working on comparative biology right now. It's one of my favorite courses," she replied with just a trace of a Southern lilt.

"I have no idea what that is," he earnestly replied.

She laughed and reassured him that not many people did, including her parents, who were simply proud she had found a passion for science early in her life. She said, "Part of it is studying the similarities of specific traits of different species as they grow from embryos. It also involves looking at the mechanisms that lead to the natural variations between species."

Spencer pretended to look sleepy, with heavier and heavier eyelids, and then plunked his head onto his laptop.

Larkin lightly pushed the top of his head. "It's really interesting!" she insisted.

He popped up with a straight back and wide eyes and promised to listen.

"So . . ." she began and then hesitated. She didn't want to embarrass herself by sharing a soliloquy of science that might end with an uncomfortable silence followed by one of them trying to make polite excuses and a swift departure. Spencer remained attentive, patiently waiting for Larkin to begin as these seeds of doubt attempted to sow themselves in her brain. She sighed, and with a small smile, she began again.

"So . . . have you ever thought about how your hands develop?" she asked, keeping her voice low so as not to disturb the others in the library.

He shook his head as she gestured for his hand. He slid into the other chair, so he was now directly facing her. She held his hand in hers and curled it into a fist. "Do you think your hands start like this, and then fingers start to pop up from the base of your hand and grow out from there, like this?" Larkin pulled each of his fingers from his closed hand.

"I honestly have never thought about that," he replied.

She noticed him looking at the silver rings on her fingers, the multicolored rope bracelet on her right wrist, and the plastic bracelet that said "Thanks, Science!" Then she opened his hand and told him to spread out his fingers. "Your hand actually starts like a paddle at first, and your fingers develop within that paddle. As the embryo grows, at some point, our hands go through a process called apoptosis where the cells in between the developing fingers are preprogrammed to die." She took her right index finger and slid it between each of his fingers as her left hand held his wrist.

"If that didn't happen, we'd have hands that looked more like a frog's. The same process happens with toes. But," she paused. She let go of his hand and animatedly held both of hers next to her face, palms toward him, as if she were beckoning for him to stop and listen. "Sometimes the process fails, and children can be born with webbed fingers and toes, or they might be completely fused together. I've always wondered if that would make them faster swimmers." She tapped her chin with her finger, pondering the thought. She continued excitedly. "Did you know some people can have three or more nipples?"

"Well, now this class is getting more interesting." Spencer grinned.

"People. Men *and* women."

"Oh . . ." he said with feigned disappointment as his shoulders dropped. He gave her a wry smile.

"When we are developing as embryos, there's an area called the milk line that grows from our armpits to our groin, and it has several areas where nipples form," Larkin continued as she traced her finger down the side of her body. "In most humans, those areas regress very early in development, leaving only two, but in some people, one or two extra may not completely go away. If it doesn't, it can look like a mole below one of the normal nipples. And guys have nipples because this area forms during development even before your sex is determined. And," Larkin said, whispering as loudly as possible, "some women with a third nipple can even lactate from that nipple! It can produce milk if there are some remnants of breast tissue there. There are lots of celebrities who have supernumerary nipples. Harry Styles has two extra ones!"

Spencer looked incredulous.

"A lot of people don't even know they've been walking around all their life with a third nipple. Lift up your shirt."

"What?"

"Let me see if you have extra nipples."

"Would that be good or bad?"

"Neither." She grinned. "Just curious."

Spencer glanced around the library. The other students were focused on their laptops and books. He lifted his T-shirt while Larkin leaned forward and inspected his torso.

"Nope. Just two." She sighed and gave him a playful frown.

He pulled down his shirt and looked at her with wonder. "You really love studying this, don't you?"

"Yes, I do. It's amazing to me how species look so similar when we first start developing, but our DNA signals determine which species will have feathers, which will have fur, which will have scales. But we start out looking so much alike. How does that happen? Why did it happen? Did you know we even start out with tails when we are embryos? They go away at about eight weeks of development, and all we are left with is a tailbone."

"How boring. I'd love to have a long tail!"

"I know, right?"

As Larkin had learned about the similarities between embryos of different species, she simply couldn't deny the argument in favor of evolution—it seemed so logical to her. She told Spencer that she and her best friend had resoundingly lost a classroom debate in high school when they'd defended evolution over creationism. Her biology teacher had praised her after class for giving a strong argument but hoped she would understand creationism better after her class went on a field trip to the Creation Museum in Kentucky the following week.

Spencer told her the Scopes Monkey Trial had been held over a hundred years ago in the town where he grew up, and residents there still pronounced evolution as "evil-lution."

Larkin's experience in high school had left her undeterred and only fueled her interests. She told Spencer she'd always pictured herself working in a lab surrounded by microscopes and books, and she already had a bench research job lined up with the university's Department of Genetics and Development after graduation. She was going to work in a lab with Dr. James Davis studying mandibular osteogenesis and facial morphogenesis.

Spencer jokingly accused her of making up random words.

She clarified that she would be working with a researcher to investigate the development of facial malformations, specifically cleft palate and cleft lip.

"He's studying the development of beaks in chickens because there are so many similarities between chicken and human development, so it is a good model to use," she explained. "Chickens can get cleft palates, and they can also get something called parrot beak where their lower jaw grows too large, like an underbite." She continued, "My mom and I were both born with underbites called mandibular prognathism. She had to have her jaw broken and wired shut for six weeks when she was a teenager. I just had to have braces, thank goodness. So, I have a personal interest in this research as well. And the PhD doc I'm going to work with is amazingly cool. He's incredibly intelligent and supportive. He has to be a genius. He is very intimidating to talk to because he's so smart."

"Wow! I'm impressed. You really have your life all thought out."

"Career goals, absolutely. Other than that, I'm still figuring things out. But what about you? Now that I've told you everything about what I'm studying, what's your major? It must be different since we've not had any classes together." She motioned to his calculator. "Are you an engineering major?"

"Oh, no. I'm a math major with a minor in business management, but my plan is to get my master's and be an actuary."

"You actually want to be an actuary?"

He chortled. "Yes, why?"

"I'm just kidding. I don't even know what that is. I just like saying 'actually' and 'actuary.'"

Spencer laughed. "Got it. Most people don't know what I'm doing, either. Actuarial science is the study of the financial impact of uncertain future events. I'll be studying how to quantify and manage risk, primarily in the fields of life and health insurance, pensions, employee benefits, and investment."

Larkin started fluttering her eyelids, then she pretended to hit her head on her laptop.

"Very funny, Larkin. It's *actually* very interesting to me. It involves a lot of mathematical calculations, which I enjoy, and making a best guess on risk. It's like being a fortune teller, but using probability and statistics instead of a crystal ball." He paused and leaned back in his chair. "And it is a good-paying career, but the credentialing and exam process is pretty rigorous. The exams are as hard as the medical boards for doctors or passing the bar for lawyers, which is intimidating. And not that getting paid well in life is everything, but I hope to be rewarded for hard work. After graduation next year, I'm hoping to start in the master's program here."

That afternoon in the library, they talked for hours about their lives and interests. Both shared a love of Americana music as well as '70s and '80s rock. They also enjoyed hiking, kayaking, and searching for the best street taco food truck. Both were introverts but never feared speaking out when they felt strongly about something. They believed in finding work that you love but having friends and hobbies that you loved more. Each wanted to live outside of a city and have a small amount of land. Spencer wanted to have his own vegetable garden, and Larkin wanted to raise chickens someday. They disagreed about pets—she was strongly pro-cat, but Spencer was solidly pro-dog. And they both wanted to have children someday, but not until their thirties.

It was starting to get late, and they decided they really needed to study. When Spencer was occupied with entering data into his calculator, Larkin picked up her phone, pretending to be checking her hair. She snapped a picture the moment Spencer glanced up. Unfortunately, her phone wasn't on silent like she thought it was. It made the telltale shutter noise, exposing Larkin's ruse. Spencer smiled broadly when he heard it. Larkin immediately looked down as her long, light brown hair fell around her face to cover the red flush rising in her cheeks. She turned her phone to silent.

Once her phone was hidden under the table, she sent her best friend the photo with the caption "future husband."

CHAPTER 3

It's estimated that between 10 to 20 in 100 known pregnancies (10 to 20 percent) end in miscarriage. Most miscarriages—8 out of 10 (80 percent)—happen in the first trimester before the 12th week of pregnancy.
—March of Dimes

Spencer and Larkin married in late summer the year after they met, just months after their graduation. It was a small ceremony at his parents' home in East Tennessee, with just a few friends and family members present. They used the money their parents had offered them for a larger wedding to make a down payment on a small ranch house on two acres of land a thirty-minute drive from Larkin's new job.

When they got back from their honeymoon in the Blue Ridge Mountains, Spencer immediately started graduate school. He would study on the same sprawling university campus where they'd met and where Larkin would work in the lab as a research assistant. She wanted to pursue her doctorate someday but planned to work for a few years while she paid down her undergraduate loans and Spencer completed his degree.

During her first day on the job, she went to the Human Resources department to get her identification badge, which listed her title as "Research Assistant I." After completing the direct deposit forms and paperwork for health insurance, vision, and dental, she walked across campus to the lab. She hadn't been there since interviewing a year earlier and was looking forward to seeing her supervisor again.

She would be trained by Susan, a Research Associate III. Susan greeted Larkin wearing a traditional white lab coat, its top pocket stuffed with pens and a pair of reading glasses. Susan had worked with Dr. Davis for more than fifteen years and had coauthored more than thirty articles relating to embryonic growth and development. She'd helped him submit multiple grants for their research and coordinated the projects for visiting international graduate students. She told Larkin she was relieved to finally have help.

Susan showed Larkin to her desk and lab station. She would have her own cubicle and computer in the middle of the lab. Several windows brought soft sunlight into the room, and throughout the lab were multiple workstations for performing experiments. Larkin would have her own workspace as well, but the team shared microscopes and photography equipment. The space was clean and quiet, with others diligently working.

Susan introduced Larkin to the international graduate students who would be there for the next year, working on their individual research projects. Abdullah, from Iran, stopped pipetting a light pink substance onto a microscope slide to turn and greet Larkin. Alondra, who was from Spain, was using a microscope with an attached camera to photograph her work. Kai came from China, and he was in his cubicle typing up an abstract for publication. They all gave her a friendly welcome. All three of them hoped to have something to publish at the end of the year.

Smiling and pointing to Larkin, Susan warned them not to use the "newbie" for their own work. She had seen it happen before with students who had struggled to make their research deadlines.

"Larkin works for Dr. Davis, not you," she reminded them. They all smiled, nodded, and promised with a little salute. Larkin was impressed that Susan had trained them so well.

After the tour, Susan took Larkin to lunch at the university food court. When they sat down to share hummus and dolmas and eat pita sandwiches, Larkin asked Susan if she had always wanted to do basic science research.

"Actually, no," Susan began. "I was in medical school and had planned to be a radiologist, but I had three miscarriages. One at nine weeks, one at thirteen weeks, and one at twelve weeks in the first three years of school. No reason to explain it medically. I was poked and prodded and tested, and no one could tell us why. My husband and I decided it might be the stress of medical school, so I quit."

"Oh. I am so sorry. That must have been awful."

"It was. And then I had to figure out what to do with the rest of my life with a biology degree. I looked into food inspection, but after a tour of a fast-food plant to see how the hamburger was processed . . . just, ugh. I'll never eat fast-food burgers again," she said, scrunching her face in disgust.

"And then I looked into research and found this job. Dr. Davis is amazing. Great mentor. Smart man. And here I am. He's very laid-back but expects professionalism and quality work. I never feel pressured by him, though. I always want to do a good job because disappointing him would feel like disappointing my father. He would never tell me if I let him down, but I would never want to feel I had. It would kill me, ya know?"

Larkin nodded as she wiped tzatziki from her mouth.

"And then, during my first year of working, I had another miscarriage. Again at thirteen weeks."

"Oh, no!" Larkin gasped.

"Yep. It's okay. That's how I found out it wasn't the stress of medical school. It was me. Or us. Or just wasn't meant to be. But

I didn't want to go back. I enjoy what I do, and I'm happy now. My husband's happy. And we have three spoiled fur babies that we love and keep us busy."

Susan opened her phone and showed Larkin pictures of three well-fed cats lounging lazily on a couch with Susan's husband. She pointed to each of the tabby cats. "That's Flynn and that's Oscar, the two black-and-gray tabbies. And that's Cindi, the orange one. They're all strays we found on our walks in the neighborhood. My husband is scared to walk with me anymore because I keep bringing them home." She let out a guffaw.

"He's right," Susan continued. "If I find another one, it's coming home with me. My dream would be finding a kindle of kittens. My husband would pretend to be upset, but he'd let me keep them. He's terrible at saying no. Fortunately, I just want cats and not expensive jewelry or elaborate vacations."

"Absolutely! He should be thanking you," Larkin agreed.

"You need to figure out one thing you can't live without, and don't let Spencer tell you no. Later, make sure you tell him that you learned some sound marriage advice today for you newlyweds." Susan wagged a finger motherly at Larkin as she spoke.

Larkin promised. "Oh, I will definitely do that. I guess I need to figure out what I really want first."

After lunch, they went to a smaller room near the lab and Susan started teaching Larkin what she would be doing daily. On the table sat a contraption that made a soft humming noise and had a temperature probe on the outside. Susan opened the front door and showed Larkin the two dozen or so chicken eggs that were slowly turning inside, as if they were on a small carnival ride.

"These are all white leghorn chicken eggs, which we get shipped to us every few weeks. We label them with the dates they arrive. We keep the eggs at 37.5 degrees Celsius with about 50 percent humidity. This incubator has got to be at least fifty years old, but Dr. Davis likes it, and it works, so we've never replaced it." She shrugged. "At two to three days, we check for viability. They are all sold to us fertilized, but some will be duds," Susan said as she washed her hands in the small sink. "Eggshells are porous, so you always want to handle them with clean hands. We don't want to transfer bacteria to the embryo."

She removed one of the eggs, dated three days ago, and took what looked like a flashlight from the table. She explained, "This is a candling lamp that we use to check on the growth of the embryo. Years ago, farmers used an actual candle to check for viable eggs, but now you can buy these gadgets online for twenty bucks."

Susan asked Larkin to turn out the lights. She held the egg above the lamp, which she turned on. The egg glowed an amber color, and veins coursed through it, leading to a darker spot in the middle.

"See that?" Susan asked, pointing to the spot. "That's our developing embryo. This one goes back to the incubator."

Susan took out several more that were healthy. But two had no vessels, and the only thing visible was the yolk floating in the albumen. "These are duds, but we call them breakfast. You can take them home if you'd like. They are some of the freshest, most delicious eggs you'll ever eat."

Then Susan candled another egg. "Now this one," she said. "This one started to develop but died."

She showed Larkin a black ring that went through the egg's inner circumference. It was called a blood ring. "These need to be disposed of or they will continue to rot. This is the avian equivalent of a miscarriage." Susan paused and asked Larkin to turn the lights back on. Susan turned her back to Larkin and set down the candling lamp. She stood quietly by the sink for a moment and then washed her hands again. She used the paper towel to wipe her nose and eyes. When she turned back to Larkin, she gave her a quick smile.

"Well, that's enough for your first day. Why don't we call it a day for you, and I'll see you back in the morning, okay?"

"Yes, of course. Thank you for everything today. I'm really looking forward to tomorrow."

Spencer picked up Larkin at the front of her building. He'd had a great first day in his master's program, but he only wanted to know about Larkin's day. She excitedly told him about her office, her workstation, her coworkers, and Susan. She told him about the chicken eggs and all the omelets and quiches they were probably going to be eating.

"It's been a long but good day for both of us," he said. "I want you to tell me more about this tonight. I just want to relax and hear your voice, okay? It will be the perfect end to the day."

Larkin and Susan started the next day in the small room with the incubator. They collected eggs from the incubator that Susan had checked a couple of days ago since they were now five days old. Back at Larkin's workstation, which included a glass hood with a door that folded up, Susan flipped a switch on the side. The fan over the hood came on. Then she grabbed a book from a nearby shelf, *Hamburger and Hamilton's Staging Series,* written in 1951. Susan and Larkin took seats on rolling stools in front of the workstation. "Okay," Susan said as she opened the book and flipped through the pages. "This is the ultimate resource for chicken embryo staging. Drs. Hamburger and Hamilton compiled photographs and drawings from forty-six chronological stages of the approximately twenty-one-day incubation period of the eggs. They wrote very detailed descriptions to accompany the illustrations, so we can make sure we are appropriately staging our samples."

She stopped on a dog-eared page and used her pen to tap an image of a chicken embryo. "We sacrifice these chicks at around five days of incubation because that is the time when the facial features we're interested in are forming, and we can compare it to the developing human embryo. We can make hypotheses on cleft lip and palate formation and the processes involved based on our experiments and observations."

After putting on a pair of gloves, she cracked an egg into a petri dish under the hood. The yolk and white spread in the dish, revealing an almost translucent embryo curled in the shape of the letter C, less than an inch in size. Dark gray eyes were developing along with tiny limb buds and a red spot that would later become the heart. Susan showed Larkin how to compare the embryo to the photos and descriptions. The first one perfectly matched the book's reference image for the desired stage. She then opened a box of scalpel blades and cut off the head.

She glanced at Larkin, who frowned and furrowed her brow. Susan set down the scalpel. "Larkin," she said. "Do you eat chicken?"

"Yes, I love chicken."

"It comes nicely packaged in plastic wrap at the grocery store, doesn't it?"

"Yes. I know what you're going to say."

"Maybe you think I'm a hypocrite, but I couldn't work in a lab that did experiments on mice or rats or rabbits. But I do eat chicken, and I'm not the one working in a plant tasked with killing chickens. My experience is completely sterilized for me by people who work a very hard job." Susan smiled kindly. "So, I'm not vegetarian or vegan, and I personally believe chickens and eggs provide an excellent source of nutrition. And these embryos provide a lot of useful information for us to better understand human development and find answers to why birth defects occur so that, hopefully, we can help prevent them. It's not my favorite part of the job, but it's for the greater good. Will you be okay with that?"

"Yes, I will. I guess I thought the embryo samples we study would come to us already processed and ready, like going to the store. That's my own ignorance. I get it. It's totally okay."

"Great. Let's let you try this now."

Susan had Larkin crack and stage the remaining embryos. They placed the dissected heads in small plastic cylinders and covered them in a thick, viscous substance. They used small forceps to move the heads very gently into the correct position for the later steps. Susan put on thicker gloves and used long tongs to grab the edge of the cylinders, then dipped them in a container of liquid nitrogen to flash freeze them. After labeling them and wrapping them in aluminum foil, they placed them into the lab freezer.

"Great job, Larkin. Why don't you take a lunch break and we'll meet here again in the afternoon?"

Larkin grabbed her purse and the lunch she'd packed and headed for the break room. As she dug through her purse to find money for a drink from the decades-old vending machine, she found her birth control pack. She looked at it and noticed she was on the last day of her placebo week. She suddenly realized she hadn't started her period yet—normally, she started on the first or second day of taking placebos. She had been so busy with coming back from the honeymoon and starting her new job that it had slipped her mind.

She left her lunch on the table, grabbed her purse, and ran down the stairs.

CHAPTER 4

Larkin walked at a fast clip to the closest pharmacy. Her head was swimming with thoughts as she tried futilely to calm down.

I'm on the pill. It's 99 percent effective when taken correctly. It's always worked before. I did miss a couple of days when I was preparing for the wedding and the honeymoon, but I always doubled up the next day like the package insert instructed. Spencer did stop using condoms a few months before we got married. But I was still on the pill! Maybe I've just been under stress with graduation and the wedding and the new job, and I've just skipped a period. Maybe that's all it is.

At the pharmacy, she grabbed a pregnancy test off the shelf, used the self-checkout, and was out of the store in under two minutes.

On the way back to the lab, as she walked with the same sense of urgency, her mind continued racing. *Oh, my God. How will Spencer react? We want kids but hadn't planned on having them this soon. He's in graduate school! My income alone can't support a child! And what is Dr. Davis going to say? I just started this job, and now I might have to tell him I'm going to have a baby?*

She ran up the stairs to the lab's fourth floor and locked herself in the bathroom. Breathing heavily from the trip upstairs, she ripped open the package, and its contents spilled onto the floor. Grabbing the foil wrapper that contained the test, she tore open one end and removed the purple cap from the plastic test stick and went into the accessible stall. With shaking hands, she held the stick between her legs as she squatted over the toilet and started to urinate. When she was done, she replaced the cap and jerked up her pants. She threw open the stall door, banging it loudly against the wall. She then made her way to the bathroom counter and laid the test down.

As she gazed at the white ceiling tiles and dusty incandescent bulbs, she zipped and buttoned her pants. Then she closed her eyes and focused on her breathing. Slow, deep breaths in through her nose and out through her mouth.

Once she felt calmer, she looked at the counter. There were, without any doubt, two lines on the test, one with a plus sign below it.

She grabbed a couple of paper towels and stuffed the test into her purse before going back to the empty break room and tossing her uneaten lunch in the trash. She focused on breathing and listening to the soft ticking of the clock over the door as she sat with her head in her hands and her elbows resting on the table.

Oh, my God . . . I'm not ready to be a mom, am I? At twenty-two? I can't have a baby now. I know Spencer will support me. That's the right decision. Right? But when is "ready"? It's going to be okay either way. Either way? What if I decide to have a baby? That would be okay, too . . . right? There are lots of mothers my age. Why not? My choice. My choice. What's my choice? Fucking hell . . .

When her lunch hour ended, Larkin went back to the lab. She set her purse on the desk, making sure the top was securely zipped, and stood motionless as she stared at the top of her bag.

"Have a good lunch?" Susan asked as she walked across the lab to Larkin's desk. "Lemme guess. Chicken salad? Egg salad? Chicken and dumplings? Chicken parmesan?" she teased.

Larkin turned with a start, gave a half-hearted smile, and said, "No. I wasn't really hungry." She looked ashen and on the verge of tears.

Susan gave her a look of concern. "Oh, I am so sorry, Larkin. I was being insensitive."

"No, no, no! It's not about that at all. I truly am fine with everything. I'm just a bit preoccupied. My stomach is a little upset."

"Would you like to go home?"

"No, thank you so much. I'll be fine."

"Well, okay, then. Please let me know if you need a break. We're going to work on how to get the specimens we froze onto microscope slides for the experiments."

Susan removed from the freezer one of the specimens they'd prepped that morning. She took it out of its foil wrapping and flipped down a glass window on the rotary cryostat machine that sat in the corner of the lab next to a rolling stool. It was about the size and shape of a small ATM and maintained a temperature of -5 degrees Celsius. After sitting down on the stool, she tapped the frozen specimen out of the plastic container into her hand and mounted it—facing her—on what she called a chuck inside the machine.

Susan then showed Larkin the handle on the machine's side. "Now, as you turn this handle, the specimen on the chuck will advance forward in very small increments. We start slicing the sample to a thickness of ten micrometers. This part goes fast because we have to slice through a decent amount of the mounting gel to get to the sample." She started moving the handle in forward circular motions as thin pieces fell to the bottom of the machine.

"You'd think I'd get frostbite doing this, but I never wear gloves. It's really not bad," Susan said as she quickly sliced. "Ah! Now we are just getting to the eyes," she said as two dark spots became visible on the specimen. "Just a little bit more until we start seeing the part of the facial structures we want."

Susan explained to Larkin what the samples they collected should look like. As Susan continued to slice the sample, they could now see the features that would develop into the nostrils and the mouth. Then Susan grabbed a microscope slide and a small paintbrush from a countertop next to the machine. She made another slice, using the paintbrush to coax the sample onto the slide in one smooth stroke.

"It takes a lot of practice to get it onto the slide flat and unwrinkled. I expect you to mess up a lot. A lot! But we will give you plenty of practice."

Susan collected about ten slides she was happy with and stored them in the freezer for later use.

"So, tomorrow we'll let you start practicing. Right now, let's head up to Dr. Davis's office, and we can tell him how you are doing. He's been so busy, he hasn't had a chance to talk to you yet."

"Now? I'm going to see him now?" Larkin stammered. The pit in her stomach had gone away for a bit while she'd focused on learning the cryostat technique, but that feeling had quickly returned.

"Yes, Larkin. Right now. Is your stomach bothering you again?"

"No, no. I'm fine. I want to see him."

Susan regarded her skeptically—Larkin was beginning to look pale again. "Okay, if you say so. Follow me."

They walked up to Dr. Davis's office on the fifth floor. The door was open, and he was on the phone. His feet were on the table, ankles crossed, as he talked to a colleague in a research laboratory at another university.

Every surface of his office was covered in stacks of books and journals on topics like genetics, histology, embryonic development, DNA sequencing, and evolutionary biology. There were at least a dozen empty coffee cups scattered about the room, some balanced precariously on books.

In a "Happy Kwanzaa" frame, there was a picture of Dr. Davis hugging a man who looked like a senior version of himself—white hair and a big smile. In another was a blurrier photo of Dr. Davis as a toddler, sitting on his dad's lap on a plaid couch, both with the same wide smiles on their faces. There was one more photo, this one of a bride and groom. It was dated in cursive script at the bottom: May 22, 1985. It looked like his dad again, this time posing with his new bride. Larkin didn't see any more photos of her in the office.

Dr. Davis hung up the phone and stood to shake Larkin's hand. "Welcome! Welcome! We are so happy to have you as part of the team, Larkin. I hope you're enjoying it so far."

They all sat, and she assured him that she was very happy with her new job. She also praised Susan's patience and teaching skills.

"She is the best. She keeps me organized," Dr. Davis agreed.

"You seem to have a lot to organize!" Larkin exclaimed and immediately regretted it, thinking she had insulted his chaotic environment.

"You mean this mess?" He laughed, looking around his office. "Never!"

Susan grumbled good-naturedly, "Believe me, I've tried."

"Oh, no . . . I didn't mean your office! I meant all your research projects. You sure seem to have a lot of irons in the fire!" Larkin then thought to herself, *Irons in the fire! Jesus, Larkin. Who says that anymore? Blacksmiths from the 1500s? Why don't you just tell him you have a bun in the oven, too?* She wanted to bury herself under a stack of his journals to hide her embarrassment.

"It's very true, yes. Lots of irons in the fire. That's a perfect idiom. I love it. And that's why you're here. I have a lot of projects going on at once. Many irons. Many fires. One of those fires is in my belly, and I know you have it, too, Larkin. That's why I hired you." He leaned forward and pointed his index finger toward her.

Still embarrassed and distracted, she only partially heard him. "Wait, what did you say is in my belly?" Her heart raced as she absentmindedly put her hands on her stomach, then quickly moved them to her sides.

"The fire, Larkin, the fire! You've got that determination to succeed! I knew it the first time I met you."

She breathed a sigh of relief. "Thank you so much, Dr. Davis. That's so nice of you to say."

"You don't need to thank me for speaking the truth."

Susan told him they should clean the lab before heading out for the day. Larkin was relieved they were about to leave his office.

"We will get together at least once a week to go over your progress, but anytime you need anything, I'll make myself available, alright?" Dr. Davis assured her.

Larkin simply nodded and decided it was best not to say anything else. She and Susan headed back to the lab to clean up their work area. Once they were at Larkin's desk, Susan told Larkin to go home and rest, adding that she hoped Larkin felt better tomorrow.

CHAPTER 5

Larkin and Spencer hadn't had time to buy much furniture for their new home, but they had two comfortable barstools in the kitchen where they always sat to eat dinner and talk about their days. Larkin's purse sat at the end of the kitchen counter. Her body was angled away from it, but she couldn't forget what was inside, hastily wrapped in paper towels. She had decided what she wanted to do.

When they were close to finishing their meal, Larkin put down her utensils and turned to Spencer. "Susan said something funny a couple of days ago," she blurted out.

"What'd she say?"

"She said that for us to have a happy marriage, I should be able to choose one thing I want, and you can't tell me 'no.'"

"Uh-oh. How much is this going to cost me?" He looked at her with skepticism.

"Umm . . . I think about three hundred thousand dollars." Larkin laughed nervously.

Spencer thought for a moment. "So . . . you want a Tesla Roadster? I didn't even know you liked cars that much," he said with bemusement.

"No, I don't want a car."

"Anything you want, Larkin. Tell me and we'll figure it out."

"I want a baby."

"Well, sure. We both want a baby someday. Maybe two or three."

"I want a baby now . . . please."

Spencer stood up from his stool, dropped his napkin, and said with a wide grin, "Great! Let's start practicing some more! Now, *that's* the key to a happy marriage!" He held her hand gently, trying to coax her toward the bedroom.

Larkin pulled him back to her and put one hand on his. "I'm pregnant."

Spencer looked into her eyes, and she repeated herself. "I'm pregnant, and I want this baby," she said.

She took the pregnancy test out of her purse and showed it to him. "I just found out today, and I didn't realize how much I wanted this until it happened, and I know this isn't the best timing, and we can't afford it right now, and I am so sorry, Spencer, but please, don't tell me no. This is the thing. Our baby. This is the one thing I want." She couldn't look at him, so she put her head down and stared at her lap.

Spencer put his hands on her cheeks and raised her face to look at him. "Larkin, I would never say 'no' to this. Ever. Okay?"

She started sobbing. "Thank you, Spencer. Thank you so much. I'm so very sorry."

"Sorry for what? Did you steal some sperm from me while I was sleeping? I don't know how you did it, but I'm impressed. Didn't even notice. You're welcome to try doing that again anytime. I'll pay more attention next time around." As he smiled, he exposed the little chip in his tooth that Larkin had fallen in love with at the library.

Relieved, Larkin wiped away her tears. "You're really not mad?"

"Mad? Why? This is good news. Surprising news, yes. But great news. Our parents are going to be excited. We can do this. Now, you are probably right about how much babies cost to raise. That may even be an underestimate, but we have eighteen years to spread out those costs. And you know how much I love crunching numbers, so you know we can figure this out."

She grabbed Spencer and squeezed him tightly. "I really had no idea how much I wanted this. I'm so happy to be having a baby with you."

"I am, too. This is really fantastic. When should we tell our parents?"

"Let's wait until the first obstetrician's appointment. Oh, my God . . . we need an obstetrician!" Larkin said, still processing their new reality. "I want to make sure everything is okay first. Susan was telling me about having multiple miscarriages, so I'll feel better having an appointment before we tell anyone."

"Of course. We can wait. So, by the way, what is Susan's 'one thing'?"

"Cats! Lots of cats!" Larkin laughed and squeezed his arm. "She said she wants to find a—what did she say?—a kindle of kittens."

"Well, maybe we need a whole flock of babies then. A bevy of babies! Or a gaggle. Or a herd. Or a clutch. Or a conspiracy, like lemurs. Or a murder, like crows," Spencer mused.

"Let's not have a murder of babies. That sounds like a horror movie. Let's just start with a baby. Singular."

As they lay in bed that night, Larkin couldn't believe how quickly her life had changed. She wanted to share her news with someone else, so she texted Aubrey, who was now in her first year of medical school:

are you awake?
always. studying. u ok?
i'm going to need you to hurry up to be my obstetrician
lol. when?
in about nine months

CHAPTER 6

September 14, 2032
The Tennessean
Conservative pro-life candidate campaigns for US Senate on platform of nationwide ban on all abortions from time of conception and banning birth control

Spencer had accompanied Larkin to her first obstetrician visit. They'd found the doctor when Larkin had asked Susan for a recommendation. Larkin had claimed she wanted to establish with someone new for birth control—a white lie since she and Spencer had agreed to tell their families about the pregnancy before telling anyone else.

The visit was routine and all good news. Dr. Parrish had estimated Larkin's due date and took a complete family history. She'd also had some routine labs drawn and prescribed prenatal vitamins. Finally, she'd told Larkin to limit caffeine and not to drink any alcohol. Spencer was excited for Larkin's next appointment the following month, when she was twelve weeks pregnant, for an ultrasound where they should be able to hear the heartbeat.

Spencer got permission from Larkin to share the news of the pregnancy when he interviewed for jobs—he wanted to work so he could help save for a small nest egg prior to the baby's arrival.

Since he was only looking for a part-time position and had no experience, they thought it might help his chances of getting hired, and it did.

Spencer was hired by a privately owned local insurance agency to help with expense reports and account reconciliation. The owner was a gregarious man with a booming voice who was a natural salesman, always ready with a firm handshake and a good, clean joke. He would know and remember your children's names, the college you attended, and your church's denomination after just one conversation.

Jack Montgomery had grown up in the area and bought the insurance franchise with his parents' generous help when he was just twenty-two years old. He had been in the business for more than three decades. He'd married when he was twenty and had a family of five. Jack had felt a connection with Spencer when he learned he had married recently and was already starting a family.

Jack was running for the US Senate and had served as a school board representative when his children were younger. He'd wanted to preserve traditional values in the school system, helped to eliminate any teaching of critical race theory, and restricted the discussion of LGBTQ topics in elementary and middle schools. He felt his views were worthy of a larger audience in Washington, DC.

Jack's office looked more like a campaign headquarters than an insurance agency. His name was plastered on red, white, and blue posters on the windows and walls. His employees all wore American flag pins on their lapels or sweaters with "I Back Jack!" pins below them. Spencer hadn't seen that many American flags in one place since he had been a kid visiting Arlington National Cemetery on Memorial Day.

Jack enjoyed telling Spencer stories about his success in the insurance industry. He told him it was an important job, making sure families have peace of mind and helping them achieve their goals. He tried convincing Spencer to reconsider his career choice.

"C'mon, Spence. Don't you think you'll get tired of sitting back with an abacus all day thinking about numbers?"

"I think actuarial science fits my personality well, sir," Spencer politely replied. *And no one uses an abacus anymore,* he thought.

"I don't think your personality is boring, son, but that's what it sounds like to be *tappity-tap-tapping* on an adding machine all day," he said as he wiggled his fingers dramatically and with a look of disdain. "Whoo. No, sir. B-O-R-I-N-G!" He craned back his head for emphasis.

"Well, I appreciate your concern, but—"

"I tell you what," Jack interrupted. "I have a new young couple coming in at two to talk about a life insurance policy. Why don't you sit in and see what it's like to give a family peace of mind? Very rewarding, very rewarding. Can't do that punching a calculator. You're not giving anyone much of anything. All you're getting are calluses on your fingers."

Spencer agreed to sit in on the appointment. A young couple walked into the office promptly at 2 p.m., and Jack immediately walked over to them and gave the man a hearty handshake. They introduced themselves as Allie and Kaiden June. Allie was wearing a flowy pink flowered dress that Jack complimented.

"Lovely wife you have there!" Jack said to Kaiden and patted him on the back. He introduced Spencer and led them all into his office.

Jack sat behind his desk with Spencer seated next to him closer to the wall. The couple sat across from them, and Allie pulled out her phone. "My parents are so happy for us to take this next step," she said. "They have been nagging us to get life insurance ever since we had our two-year-old. If you don't mind,

I'm going to record this for them. I don't think they will believe we are finally doing this."

"Go right ahead. Your parents have a lot to be proud of. You're on the right track," Jack said. "Have you researched whole versus term life? Do you have an idea of what you'd like?" Allie continued to video record.

"We'd like term policies for the whole family," Kaiden told him, and Allie nodded in agreement.

"Oh! You'd like a policy for the two-year-old as well? We can do that. They are relatively inexpensive. I know it's a tough reality to think about losing your child, but it's a responsible decision. Your parents raised you right." He grinned widely as he looked at Allie's phone and gave a thumbs-up.

Jack continued, "I'd recommend a whole life insurance policy for your son. That way it will build up some cash value, and he can borrow against it when he's older for unexpected expenses." He turned to Spencer and winked. It looked like he was going to sell three policies at once today, showing Spencer how he could expertly close a deal.

"That sounds wonderful," Kaiden said. "Can we see rates for term life for Allie and myself and whole life for our son and the new baby?" He gestured to Allie's belly.

Jack smiled widely. "Congratulations! Well, of course, but we'll wait on writing up a policy on your other child until after he or she is born. How far along are you, if you don't mind me asking?"

"Oh, I'm only seven weeks along. I'm not even sure if it's a boy or a girl yet, but I think it's a girl. We are just so excited already. I went ahead and got out all my old maternity clothes!"

Jack laughed. "Well, I appreciate your forethought, but we don't write policies until after the baby is born. You understand, right?"

"Well, no, we don't," Kaiden said.

"This is *life* insurance, right?" Allie asked.

"Yes, it's life insurance. That's what we have been talking about and what you came in for, right?" Jack answered. Spencer could tell Jack was growing agitated even though his voice remained calm, just like a seasoned politician's.

"Well, our daughter is a 'life,' wouldn't you agree, Mr. Montgomery?" Allie pressed.

Jack answered matter-of-factly. "Yes, she is a life in the eyes of God," he said, narrowing his eyes. He crossed his arms over his chest and sat back in his chair with a look of derision.

"Well, then we would like a life insurance policy for her as well. Today," Kaiden said seriously.

Spencer knew this conversation had taken a bad turn. He tried to push his chair as far into the corner as he could so he wouldn't be visible on the recording.

"We don't write life insurance policies on babies that don't exist yet," Jack said flatly.

"You're saying our baby doesn't exist? That our baby is not *really* a life yet? Is that what you are saying?" Allie questioned.

"We thought you believed life begins at conception, Mr. Montgomery. Shouldn't you start issuing policies at that moment?" Kaiden asserted.

"What if I have a miscarriage tomorrow? Does my baby not deserve to have her funeral expenses covered by insurance? Is this life not of value to you?" Allie asked.

Jack abruptly stood. "Turn off that phone, and get out of my office. You two are nothing but scheming liberal scum trying to make a stupid argument with your 'gotcha' tactics. Get out. Get out now!" He made a grab for Allie's phone, but she snatched it away and continued recording. His office staff helped corral the couple to the front door.

"Why do you get to define what a life is when it's convenient for you?" Kaiden shouted. "Why do you get to decide what women can do with their bodies? What gives you that right?"

Allie joined in. "And now you want to ban birth control to give women even less control of their reproductive rights? When will it end? Can a guy pull out anymore, or will you try to ban that next?"

Jack's face was red with rage. He continued to repeat "Get out! Get out! Get out now!" His voice rose as he walked toward Kaiden and Allie. His staff gathered behind him.

"Godless baby killers!" Jack yelled toward the front door when Kaiden and Allie had left the office. Then he turned around and said it again: "Nothing but Godless baby killers! They won't stop me from running or winning. This will give me more fortitude. We are surrounded by evil. They have only strengthened my convictions."

Jack held up his arms and proclaimed, "'Out of the mouth of babes and nursing infants You have ordained strength because of Your enemies, that You may silence the enemy and the avenger.'"

"Amen, Jack. Amen!" The staff members clasped their hands, nodded, and closed their eyes. Spencer just stared ahead, saying nothing, still in shock as to what he had just witnessed.

Within two hours, the recording of Jack Montgomery, conservative hypocrite, was trending on social media, igniting fierce debate on the definition of life, a woman's right to choose, and the fight to restore the protections of *Roe v. Wade*.

CHAPTER 7

That evening after work, as they were sitting on the couch, Spencer showed Larkin the video that had already gone viral. Fortunately, Spencer was only occasionally in the frame—just briefly—and was not recognizable.

"Oh, my God, Spencer. I had no idea he was the same guy I'd heard about in the news. You aren't going to keep working for him, are you?"

"No, of course not. I should have looked into this before I accepted the job. I can't work for him. I'll stay until I find something else. Hopefully, it won't take long. I don't want to work for him, and I certainly won't vote for him."

"I can't imagine who would vote for him. Who could possibly think banning birth control would be popular?"

"More than you'd think. He's doing really well in the polls."

"Well, maybe this experience will change his outlook?" Larkin looked at Spencer hopefully.

He said it only seemed to make Jack Montgomery more sanctimonious, if that was even possible. "Let's talk about something more fun, okay?" He changed the subject. "Are you ready to start calling our families tonight?" It had already been a week since the OB visit.

"Yes! Can we call my parents first?" Larkin asked. It was her parents' twenty-sixth wedding anniversary, and she wanted to surprise them. When they heard the news, they were elated. She was their only child, and they were ready to be grandparents.

They started suggesting names for the baby and offered to babysit anytime. Her dad was going to teach his grandchild to golf, and her mom was going to teach the baby to speak German. They'd already decided they wanted to be called Grandpa and Oma.

Larkin promised to send ultrasound pictures after they'd seen the obstetrician for the twelve-week appointment. She'd had no idea how much profound and immediate joy this news would give them. The delight continued as they called Spencer's parents and texted his siblings, aunts, uncles, and friends, promising everyone updates as soon as possible.

It wasn't long before Larkin's mother helped her to start choosing items for her baby registry and bought her books on breastfeeding and having a healthy pregnancy. Spencer's mother bought them a book of baby names with her preferred choices already highlighted.

The couple had their second appointment with Dr. Parrish a few weeks after making the announcements to their families.

"Hello, again, Larkin and Spencer," Dr. Parrish greeted as she walked into the exam room. "How are you feeling, Larkin? Any nausea? Spotting?"

Larkin said she had been feeling well and was making sure to take her prenatal vitamins, and she was drinking only half a cup of coffee a day. She also told Dr. Parrish about the books her mother had given her and reported that she had been reading about nutritional safety during pregnancy. The doctor praised her for getting off to a good start.

"I know you are both excited about today. Larkin, why don't you lie back and we will get you ready for the ultrasound?"

Spencer stood beside her and held her hand. Dr. Parrish lifted Larkin's gown and apologized for the cold, clear goo she squirted onto her lower abdomen. She rolled the ultrasound machine closer to the exam table. Placing the transducer on

Larkin's belly, she moved it back and forth while watching the screen on the machine. She quickly found the heart. They all saw it rapidly beating and heard its reassuring sound. Spencer squeezed Larkin's hand. Dr. Parrish was quiet as she kept angling and repositioning the transducer, pointing it at the ethereal image floating in the dark space that was the amniotic fluid.

Larkin found it odd that the doctor hadn't commented on anything yet. She knew the heartbeat had to be a good sign. Maybe she was trying to determine the sex.

Dr. Parrish turned from the screen to look at them. "Larkin. Spencer. Your baby's brain hasn't developed," she said, her voice low but clear.

Puzzled, Spencer asked, "Will it develop in a few more weeks?"

"No, it won't. Your baby has anencephaly. The skull and brain did not develop. I'm so sorry. This is not compatible with life."

Larkin stared at the screen in disbelief. "But I heard the heartbeat. I *saw* it beating. I don't understand."

"Yes, there is a heartbeat. The baby is still viable now, but you will either miscarry or the baby will be born stillborn. It's also possible the baby could live for a few hours or days after birth. I wish there were an easy way to say this."

"You could be wrong about this, right? Maybe you just can't see it. Maybe I didn't drink enough water before I came for you to get a good view."

"No, Larkin. I am sure. I wish I had better news for you today. I'm going to step out a moment and give you some time alone. I'll get you some information, and we can talk some more."

Dr. Parrish left Spencer and Larkin in complete shock.

"She has to be wrong, Spencer. Maybe we should get a second opinion. Maybe she's inexperienced. Maybe we should ask her if one of the other doctors could come in and look."

He started an internet search on his phone, typing in the words *baby brain not developed 12-week ultrasound.* He silently read the first result: "There is 100 percent accuracy of diagnosing anencephaly by 12-13 weeks gestation. The condition is fatal." He put his phone in his pocket and hugged Larkin as he started to weep. She started to cry softly, but it crescendoed into heaving, uncontrollable sobs.

Dr. Parrish came back in with some informational pamphlets. She tried to give them to Larkin and Spencer, but they refused to take them from her hand, as if accepting them meant accepting the awful news. She tucked them under Larkin's purse and asked that they read them later. She apologized again for having to give them such devastating news and referred them to a maternal-fetal medicine specialist for further testing and counseling.

Larkin and Spencer didn't talk on the way home. Their phones started chiming with texts from family members who knew today was the day and wanted them to send ultrasound pictures and updates. They turned off their phones for the rest of the drive.

When they got home, Larkin lay flat on her back in bed. She felt dehydrated from crying so much. She rubbed her lower belly like it was a genie's lamp. Her only wish was to make her baby healthy. Spencer lay down beside her and said he would let their families know tomorrow. She asked him to tell them not to text her or call her right now. She just couldn't talk about it yet.

Larkin woke up in the morning to the sound of her phone's alarm buzzing. She had a headache and felt like she had a terrible hangover. As she started to slowly rouse, she suddenly remembered why she felt so awful. Her recollections of the previous day made her head hurt even more. She felt as if her heart could actually break in half. She rolled over to look at her husband, who was still sleeping soundly, not wanting to wake him up so he could enjoy a little more time away from this world.

When he did wake, he looked the way Larkin felt: exhausted and heartbroken. They hugged each other tightly before they left on their morning commute. Spencer reassured her that they would get through this together but seemed at a loss for more words.

Larkin was thankful to be the only one in the lab when she arrived. She knew she couldn't talk to anyone right now. No one at work even knew she was pregnant, and she was going to keep the news private for a while longer.

She started her morning by going to the freezer and removing a few of the microscope slides containing slices of tissue specimens. She then removed the reagent she needed from the refrigerator; the reagent contained a marker that would adhere to a protein she was studying on the specimens. The protein would then fluoresce when placed under a special light on the microscope.

Dr. Davis knew this protein was important in the development of the avian embryo's facial structures—it signaled when the medial nasal, lateral nasal, and maxillary processes came together during development to form the mouth and nose. He theorized that interruptions in this signaling process led to the development of cleft lip and cleft palate.

Larkin let the slides thaw for just a few minutes while she prepared the reagent. She then drew a half milliliter of the substance into a pipette and placed it on the slide. It sat for about fifteen minutes before she tapped off the excess and brought it over to the microscope with the camera attached to the top. She then turned off the lights in the lab and sat down in front of the microscope.

When she turned on the microscope, she flipped the lens to forty times magnification and switched to the mercury-vapor bulb. She adjusted the view until the specimen came into focus, and then she moved the microscope stage, stopping when she saw the area she was interested in. It was brightly lit with thousands of pinpoint fluorescent green dots on a black background, like a monochromatic Seurat painting.

She recognized the area where the pinpoints of light were clustered together and knew they would eventually form the upper jaw and nostrils, defining the earliest beginnings of the facial structures. She took several photos to share with Dr. Davis. Larkin could also see where the eyes were starting to form—and the developing brain.

She sat back in her chair. Larkin understood why her baby's brain hadn't developed. Just as a cleft lip would occur if the areas she was studying failed to unite at the preprogrammed time, her baby's brain had never formed because, somehow, the cells had missed the developmental window when the neural tube should have closed. She remembered learning about neural tube defects like spina bifida in her embryology class a couple of years ago, and now her baby had the worst kind of defect.

She knew it could have happened for genetic reasons. Or maybe she didn't have enough folate in her system at the critical time when her baby needed it before she knew she was pregnant. She hadn't taken any medicines that would have caused it. However it happened, it had happened. She understood the science of it but couldn't understand the unfairness of it all, and she felt the overwhelming sadness start to wash over her again.

When Abdullah walked into the lab, he flipped on the lights and startled her. He saw Larkin sitting at the microscope. "Oh! My apologies, Larkin. I didn't know you were in the middle of an experiment." He walked back to turn off the lights again.

"No. It's okay. I'm done. No worries."

Larkin went to her cubicle and sat alone. If she started crying again, she wouldn't be able to stop. She thought of the baby growing inside her. Everything else would continue to grow—the heart, the lungs, the limbs would all be normal. The thought of feeling her baby kicking in a month or two filled her with a sense of dread when it gave so many other new mothers joy.

Dr. Parrish had mentioned that she might miscarry. Before her first visit, Larkin had been worried she might lose her baby as Susan had many times and as so many other women had sadly experienced. But now she selfishly hoped she would. She was ashamed of herself for even thinking it, but she didn't know how she would be able to cope with carrying the baby to term, something Dr. Parrish had said was a possibility.

Abdullah popped his head over the wall of her cubicle. "Do you mind if I borrow your lab hood for a few hours? I've got a couple of things going on at once."

"Sure. No problem at all." Larkin gave him a distracted half smile. She paused and then said, "Hey, Abdullah. Can I ask you a personal question?"

"Absolutely."

"Are you Muslim?"

"Well, my name is Abdullah, and I'm from Iran, so that's a pretty safe bet," he said good-naturedly.

Larkin replied, "Sorry if that sounded stupid. My actual personal question is more about your beliefs."

"I'll do my best to answer."

"What is the Islamic view on abortion?"

"Wow. Well, I wasn't expecting that. I thought you were just going to ask me if I eat bacon," he joked.

"You don't have to answer, Abdullah. I apologize if that was too personal."

"No, no, no. Not at all. It's pretty clear, for the most part. Abortion is generally forbidden, but if there is a threat of harm to the mother, or the fetus has anomalies incompatible with life, then it is acceptable before ensoulment."

"'Ensoulment'? When the fetus is considered a soul? When is that?"

"Yes. That's the 120th day of gestation. It's overall very consistent in the Islamic religion."

"Thank you for explaining. I was just wondering."

"Abortion in the United States is much more complicated, isn't it? Seems like everyone has an opinion, and every state has their own rules."

"Yes, that's very true, but it's only the opinion of six people that changed the law for hundreds of millions. It doesn't matter if you believe something different. It's decided by who is in power."

"Next time, maybe ask me about bacon, okay? Much easier topic."

Larkin promised. She had also made her decision.

CHAPTER 8

June 24, 2022
AP News
Supreme Court overturns *Roe v. Wade*: States can ban abortion

Larkin was thirteen in the summer of 2022 when the Supreme Court's *Dobbs v. Jackson Women's Health Organization* decision overturned *Roe v. Wade*. After that, states were free to impose any limits they wanted on abortion.

That August, Tennessee's Human Life Protection Act went into effect, banning all abortions. Exceptions to the law were made only to save the mother's life or to prevent irreversible impairment of a major bodily function.

Other states had similar "trigger laws" that went into effect immediately after the *Dobbs* decision. It was rumored that conservative states were considering even more restrictive laws to prevent women from traveling to states where abortion was still legal. Some states were even looking into banning internet searches on abortion.

Larkin's parents had been shocked that the protection they had grown up with was now gone. Their mothers had marched for a right that they thought would remain in place for their children and grandchildren.

The ramifications made national news less than a month later when it was reported that a ten-year-old girl in Ohio had been raped and impregnated. Under the new law, she was unable to get an abortion in her state because she was six weeks and three days along when she learned she was pregnant, and the "heartbeat law" in her state made it illegal. She had to travel to Indiana to have the procedure.

Larkin had been only three years older than that little girl. She couldn't imagine suffering a trauma like that. The rape itself would have been horrible enough. Being forced to carry and deliver a baby at that young age sounded scary and awful. She felt so sad for that little girl and mad at the adults who didn't know her or her family but had decided what was "right" for her.

Early in the fall of seventh grade, Larkin and her classmates attended a "family life" education program. Her parents had always been open with her about sex, contraception, homosexuality, gender identity, and consent. They knew this program was an abstinence-only course, but they agreed to let her attend if they later discussed together what she had learned.

Ten years before Larkin's class assembled in the auditorium, Senate Bill 3310, also known as the Gateway Law, was passed. It banned Tennessee public schools from discussing behaviors such as oral sex and genital touching—anything that could be considered a "gateway" to sexual intercourse.

Sex education wasn't taught in any Tennessee public schools, but if a county's pregnancy rate "exceeded 19.5 pregnancies per 100 females ages 15 to 17," per the state legislature, then those schools were required to provide a family life course discouraging "non-abstinent behavior" while strictly avoiding the topic of actual sex. Larkin lived in one of those counties in a suburb of Nashville.

The students were asked to fill out an anonymous questionnaire before the speaker began. Two of the questions asked if they'd ever had sexual intercourse, and if they hadn't, did they plan to wait until marriage to have sex?

Larkin wasn't planning to get married until she was at least thirty but doubted she would be a virgin until then. She didn't care if the questions were anonymous or not. She didn't answer and handed in a blank page. Her best friend, Aubrey, did the same but added a crude drawing of a small penis on the bottom of the form. She showed it to Larkin before turning it in, and they both giggled until their teacher, who stood near the back of the room, shushed them.

The speaker at the podium introduced herself as Mrs. Elizabeth Hawks and stated she was a certified Sexual Risk Avoidance Specialist. She looked to Larkin to be about the same age as her mom. She was dressed in a gray cardigan and a long, navy blue skirt with a small cross necklace and gold stud earrings. The necklace's serpentine chain was caught on the top button of the sweater, making the cross awkwardly dangle sideways. She wore thick, black eyeliner on the top and bottom of her eyelids, and her hair was dyed so blond it almost looked white, barely contrasting with her pale skin. Larkin thought she looked a bit like a sickly panda bear.

The school had purchased the curriculum from Make the Right Choice, a faith-based organization that taught biblically aligned sex education. Mrs. Hawks's job was to present that information to Larkin and other students across the state.

Mrs. Hawks began talking about marriage and family and commitment and healthy relationships and two-parent households and the joy of raising biological children or adopted children or both while an assistant tallied the anonymous questionnaires. Several minutes into the course, the assistant handed Mrs. Hawks a summary page with the survey results. Mrs. Hawks was pleased to announce that none of the students said they'd had sexual intercourse and 100 percent of those who'd responded planned to wait until marriage. She assured them all they were making good choices and started to clap. The teachers in attendance, and most of the students, gradually joined in the tepid applause.

Larkin put her head down at that point to keep from laughing. She had been learning about the scientific method in her biology class, along with the appropriate way to gather objective data. This was not the way.

Of course, a bunch of kids lied. Who would tell a stranger anything like that? Larkin thought, *We just told her what she wanted to hear so we wouldn't get a lecture on being a piece of used-up chewing gum or something if we don't save ourselves until marriage.* She'd heard other students had been told things like that in prior years when they'd been honest with their answers.

Mrs. Hawks continued emphasizing how sexual activity affects the whole person, including the physical, social, emotional, psychological, economic, and educational consequences of nonmarital sexual activity. She discussed how teen sexual behavior can lead to other risky behaviors such as drinking, drug use, dating violence, and sexual aggression. She encouraged students to practice refusal skills to help them resist sexual activity and gave tips on how to develop healthy relationships that result in a strong marriage.

At the end of the presentation, Mrs. Hawks asked if there were any questions. She said students could raise their hands, or they could write down their questions if they preferred.

Other than a few murmurs from restless students wanting to catch their buses home or head to after-school practices, there was silence.

Aubrey elbowed Larkin in the ribs until she raised her hand.

"Yes?"

"Hi . . . yeah . . . so . . ." Larkin took in a deep breath. "Since *Roe v. Wade* was overturned this summer by the Supreme

Court, will your organization now consider teaching safe sex and contraception to help prevent unwanted teen pregnancies since abstinence-only teaching has been proven to be ineffective?" Larkin paused and sharply inhaled as she waited for Mrs. Hawks to reply.

The auditorium was quiet other than a few random snickers. "Try-hard!" one boy shouted under a cupped hand, resulting in an outburst of laughter from several others. Aubrey reached for Larkin's hand and gave it a reassuring squeeze.

Larkin didn't move, but her face grew hot.

When the laughter stopped, Mrs. Hawks pursed her lips and thanked Larkin for her question. "Rest assured," she said, "everything that I have discussed today is medically and scientifically sound and designed to help young adults like yourself become responsible leaders and parents in our communities in the future. Until those facts change, the content of this presentation will not change. Thank you all for your attention, and I hope you all continue to make the right choice."

She gave a quick nod, picked her notes off the podium, and walked off the stage as students began gathering their backpacks and heading out the door.

Larkin mumbled, "That didn't answer my question at all."

Aubrey whispered, "Well, I hope she liked the penis I drew for her. It's probably the only one she's seen besides her husband's."

CHAPTER 9

When Larkin was fifteen, she'd asked her mother to make an appointment with her pediatrician. She was having a lot of cramping and heavy bleeding with her periods and wasn't sure if it was normal.

At Dr. Mills's office, Larkin handed the nurse a urine specimen in a plastic cup that had her initials and birthday written on the side. Her mother sat in a chair across the room, and Larkin sat on the exam table with the crinkly white paper. The nurse held Larkin's hand, palm up, and pricked her finger to take a blood sample. Then she wiped Larkin's finger and applied a bright yellow bandage with some cartoon characters on it that Larkin didn't recognize.

A few minutes later, Dr. Mills gave a couple of quick knocks on the door and walked in with a warm smile, her laptop in hand. She talked fast but was always very thorough and kind. Larkin loved the energy packed into Dr. Mills's petite, four-foot-eleven-inch frame.

"Hi, Larkin! Great to see you again. Tell me why you're here today."

"Well . . . I've been having a lot of cramping with my periods. It's so bad that I have to take ibuprofen and use a heating pad. And the bleeding is really heavy. I have to change tampons almost every couple of hours at school, which is hard to do, and when I wake up in the morning, I've soaked through the heavy overnight pads. We have to wear white uniforms in soccer sometimes, and I've bled through a couple of times, which is gross."

"Well, let's see what I can do to help," Dr. Mills said. "I'm sure we can figure something out."

After Larkin's examination, Dr. Mills told her and her mother that Larkin could start a trial of hormone therapy to see if it made her periods lighter and eased her cramping.

"Would that mean shots?" Larkin asked.

"No, it would be a small pill you would take every day. It's 'the pill,' an oral contraceptive. A lot of young women take them to prevent pregnancy, but other women and adolescents take them for irregular periods, heavy periods, ovarian cysts, and dysmenorrhea, which is the medical term for the bad cramping you are having. Other patients are referred to me by dermatologists because the pill helps with acne. There are lots of reasons why patients take it other than to prevent pregnancy."

Dr. Mills reviewed the side effects and warned them about an increased risk of getting a blood clot, especially in women who smoke or have a family history of clotting disorders. She jokingly told Larkin that if she started on the pill, she would have to give up her cigarette habit. Larkin smiled and promised never to smoke or vape.

Dr. Mills asked Larkin's mom if she would like for her to write Larkin a prescription. Her mother replied that it was up to Larkin.

"Agreed," Dr. Mills said. "Let me talk to Larkin in private about some other things, and then I will send her back out to the waiting room with you. If she decides that's what she would like to do, I'll send a prescription to your pharmacy. After about four to six months, if she doesn't see an improvement, let me know. How does that sound?"

After Larkin's mom thanked Dr. Mills and headed to the waiting room, the doctor asked Larkin if she had any questions so far.

"Why might it take up to six months to see if I get better? That seems like a long time."

"It might not take that long. It depends on how your body responds. It might be quicker."

Dr. Mills took a Sharpie from her front pocket and drew something on the exam paper that looked like a longhorn steer. She explained that the uterus (she pointed to the steer's head) is where the menstrual blood lining builds up. The hormones should help thin this lining, but it may take some time. Dr. Mills said the pill would also stop Larkin from ovulating and pointed to what looked like Christmas ornaments hanging from the tips of the steer's horns—the ovaries and eggs.

"Did you know women are born with a couple of million eggs, Larkin?"

Larkin nodded; she remembered hearing this in her biology class.

"They are very small. Only about the size of the dot on the letter *i*," Dr. Mills continued. "It's amazing to think about, isn't it?"

Larkin agreed.

"Now, even though you'll be taking hormones to regulate your periods, they are very effective at preventing pregnancy. Are you sexually active, Larkin?"

She shook her head.

"If you decide to become sexually active, please talk to me first, okay? It's your decision, but my job is to keep you as safe and healthy as I can. You can call me if you need to talk. Anything we discuss is private and protected by doctor-patient confidentiality. I can't tell anyone anything we have discussed, including your parents, unless you are in danger of hurting yourself or someone else."

"Yes, ma'am."

"Alright, then. I hope the medicine helps you. If not, let me know."

Larkin texted Aubrey after the appointment to tell her she was going to be starting the pill.

slut, she texted back.

lmao not taking for that

whatever. i'm coming over slut

haha ok

A few hours later, Aubrey arrived at Larkin's house. As they were lying on Larkin's bed and scrolling through videos on their phones, Aubrey asked if she could also get a prescription for the pill from Dr. Mills.

"Sure. Why not?"

"She's not my doctor."

"Then see your doctor."

"I don't want my mom and dad to know. They'd never let me."

"They found out you're having sex, right? Didn't your mom see some texts?"

"Yeah . . . she and my dad yelled at me and took me to a walk-in clinic for STD testing and a pregnancy test. I can't go to Brody's house anymore. They told me we can't be in my room, especially with the door closed. They make us stay in the den when he comes over. They made me promise to never do it again, so I did."

"But you're still having sex, right?"

"Well, yeah, but they think I can be a born-again virgin. They even got me a purity ring." She held up her left hand and pointed to the silver band with cursive script that said "True Love Waits" and rolled her eyes.

"I guess they think it has retroactive power or something. It's obviously not working. Brody and I use condoms, but I really want the pill, too."

"Aubrey, that condom is going to break and you're going to get pregnant and you'll be a teen mom with a reality show who lives with her grandmother after being kicked out of her parents' house. Later, you'll be struggling to go to college and get into medical school to achieve your dream of being an obstetrician while your deadbeat boyfriend goes off to a Division I school on a full baseball scholarship and you'll have to constantly fight with him to be a dad and pay child support."

"You seem to have thought this through."

"More than you have!"

"I said I want the pill! Can you ask Dr. Mills for me?"

"Okay, since I care about you not being an idiot."

The next day, Larkin called Dr. Mills's office and left a message with her nurse. At the end of the workday, the doctor called her back.

"Hi, Larkin. It's Dr. Mills. Did you have a problem getting your prescription?"

"No, ma'am. I'm calling for a friend of mine. Doctors follow the HIPAA-cratic oath, right? Isn't that what you told me about keeping things private?"

"Well, there is a Hippocratic Oath where we promise to do our best to take good care of and not harm a patient, but do you mean doctor-patient confidentiality?"

"Yes. That's it. So, my friend wants to be on the pill like me, but she wants to take it so she won't get pregnant. But she doesn't want her parents to find out. Can she see you for that?"

"I would be happy to see her if she would like to be my patient, but sometimes parents don't allow their teens to speak with the doctor in private. And if we were able to talk in private, I couldn't tell her parents that she is having sex, but it would be difficult to keep it completely anonymous if she is getting a prescription."

Dr. Mills proceeded, "I would recommend your friend go to our county health department. They can see patients down to the age of fourteen without parental consent. They can perform STD testing, provide counseling, and prescribe birth control if they determine your friend is mature enough to consent. It's not far from your school. That would be the best way, I think. But it may not be an option for much longer, so your friend should go soon."

CHAPTER 10

According to Tennessee Supreme Court case law, minors ages 14–17 years are able to receive medical care in Tennessee without parental consent.
—Michelle Fiscus, MD, FAAP, former medical director of Tennessee Vaccine-Preventable Diseases and Immunization Program

Fired from her position after emailing this information to physicians during the COVID-19 pandemic.

Larkin texted Aubrey the information Dr. Mills had given her about the county health department. They were free to go the following Wednesday after school. Larkin didn't have soccer practice that day, and Aubrey's student government meeting was canceled. Aubrey's parents didn't know that, though, so they wouldn't expect her to be home. She texted her brother, Lance, during lunch and asked him to drive her to the health department after school.

Aubrey and Larkin met Lance at his car in the seniors' parking lot a little after 3 p.m.

"Why do you guys want to go to the health department?" he asked Aubrey as he leaned against the door of his car.

"I'm thinking of doing some volunteer work there for my health sciences requirement. I think it will look good on my college application."

"And why are you bringing Larkin?" he asked skeptically.

"Same thing."

"You want to be a doctor someday, too, Larkin?" Lance probed.

"No. I'm going to be a research scientist, but it will still look good on a college application."

"Sure it will," he said and raised one eyebrow.

"While you guys are there, can you grab me some more free condoms? That's where I get all mine." He smirked.

"Gross. Absolutely not," Aubrey replied, her face scrunched in disgust.

Larkin bent over and made retching noises.

"Whatever. Get in the car," he muttered.

When they arrived, he dropped them off at the front door. As Aubrey and Larkin stepped out of the car, Lance said, "It's good to get on birth control, Sis. You're smarter than I thought you were."

"I told you already, we are just volunteering!" Aubrey huffed and slammed the door.

The health department was a square, utilitarian, red brick building with its name in large metal letters next to the entrance door. Larkin realized she had passed it hundreds of times without noticing it. Aubrey walked to the front desk. Larkin followed, pausing several feet behind her. Aubrey told the woman seated behind the reception window that she was there because she would like to start birth control.

The receptionist told Aubrey they did take walk-in appointments, but they had been busy all day. The patient care representative would have to ask the nurse practitioner if they'd be able to see her. She told Aubrey to fill out a new-patient packet while she waited.

The girls sat down in the lobby on the dark brown plastic chairs. The white linoleum floors looked freshly polished. Aubrey started filling out the pages of paperwork on a clipboard, leaving blank spaces for health information she didn't know and couldn't ask her parents about.

Larkin got up and looked around while she waited for her friend to finish. Even though they had been friends since day care and knew everything about each other, she didn't want Aubrey to think she was reading over her shoulder as she answered questions about her number of sexual partners and vaginal symptoms.

The waiting room was filled mostly with women who had young children and babies in tow. A toddler with a runny nose and orange cracker crumbs around his mouth wandered over to Larkin and gently tried to grab her phone from her hand. She assumed the green cartoon dinosaurs on the case had caught his attention. His mother scooped him up and apologized.

On the pale yellow cinder block walls, posters depicted a baby smiling just before getting a vaccination in his thigh, a young couple holding hands above informational text on the availability of STD testing, and a pregnant woman in a pastel pink top—hands on her rounded belly—next to a reminder about the importance of folate for a developing baby's brain.

Against one wall was an oak rack containing free informational brochures on HIV prevention, family planning, breastfeeding, infant and child nutrition, and dental care. Larkin was about to grab a brochure on HPV vaccination when a nurse called Aubrey's name and told her they were able to work her into the schedule.

Larkin walked back over to Aubrey. "Do you want me to come with you?" Larkin asked.

"Nah, the fewer people looking at my 'no-no square,' the better. But thank you," Aubrey replied as she stood up and gave her friend a hug.

Larkin grinned at the memory of the silly song about the "no-no square," which they used to sing when they were little. She settled into one of the chairs in the lobby to wait for her friend.

Aubrey gave a low little wave to Larkin as she went through the door leading to the exam rooms, and Larkin held up both hands with crossed fingers.

Larkin's phone buzzed a few minutes later when Aubrey sent a picture of a clear plastic device sitting on a silver tray and a text that said *wtf??????!!!!!!!!?????* Aubrey followed up with a selfie, her face twisted in mock despair. Larkin was nervous for her friend, and she wished she could have stayed with her.

After about half an hour had passed, Aubrey came through the waiting room door. She faked a limp and held a hand to her stomach as she walked toward Larkin, who lightly punched her in the arm and told her not to scare the children who were watching her.

They walked across the street to a Mexican restaurant, where they sat in a booth, ate the free salsa and chips, and drank sodas. Aubrey also texted Lance and asked him to pick them up.

Larkin asked Aubrey about the exam while they waited.

"The lady was very nice and tried to help me calm down. It was just really weird having someone—two someones!—look that closely at me down there."

"Just think. That will be you someday, looking at a lot of strange cooches," Larkin teased. "I didn't have to do any of that. I guess because I just take the pill for my periods. Did it hurt?"

"Well, she first put that plastic duck-billed thing inside me. That was weird. It's called a speculum. It was just a little uncomfortable. And then she put in an IUD thingy that looks like a plastic letter 'T' with strings hanging off of it. That felt like a really bad period cramp." Aubrey frowned. "It still feels crampy now. And she said I'll probably have some spotting. She told me to take some ibuprofen and it should feel better. I decided to get the IUD so I don't have to worry about remembering to take a pill or my mom finding a birth control pack." She took a long sip of her drink.

"That was a good idea. I'm really glad you went, Aubrey. I don't want you being a teen mom reality star." Larkin laughed. "Did you ask her about the HPV shot?"

"No. I wanted to, but I figured if my mom finds out I went there to get birth control, it would be bad enough. If I got the HPV shot, she would completely freak out."

"Why? I got mine a few years ago. My mom wanted me to have it."

"She thinks it makes girls sterile and promiscuous." Aubrey rolled her eyes. "She already thinks I'm promiscuous, so maybe she just wants to be sure I can still give her grandkids someday. Maybe I'll just go back next year when I can drive myself."

CHAPTER 11

January 8, 2026
The Tennessean
Tennessee legislature overturns Mature Minor Doctrine. Teens 14–17 no longer able to receive health care without parental consent.

Larkin was relieved that Aubrey's parents had never found out about her IUD. The next year, she encouraged Aubrey to drive herself to the health department with her brand-new driver's license to request the HPV shot. Larkin had been reading online about the safety of the HPV vaccine. She researched what Aubrey's mom had told her about it making girls sterile and found several websites with names of organizations she didn't recognize claiming the shot caused "premature ovarian failure," which could lead to infertility, osteoporosis, estrogen deficiency, and heart disease, but the majority of information she read said it was safe and effective, and the rates of cervical cancer in young women had dropped significantly since the vaccine had been introduced twenty years ago. Larkin made Aubrey promise she would go.

After school a few days later, Larkin received a text from Aubrey. It contained a photo of a laminated sign taped to the health department door: "Effective January 8, 2026: Patients under 18 MUST be accompanied by an adult to receive services at ALL Tennessee Health Departments."

this sucks, Aubrey texted.
wow. yeah. how dumb
at least I won't be sterile like you I guess
haha

The Mature Minor Doctrine had been law in Tennessee since the 1980s, but when Tennesseans became aware of the long-forgotten legislation during the COVID-19 pandemic, Republican lawmakers demanded its repeal. They accused the health department of having an agenda and encouraging teens to defy their parents by getting vaccinated "when they don't even know what they are putting in their bodies." Although no one could find any wayward teens who were surreptitiously trying to get a COVID-19 shot, the law was still overturned, ending all health care services for teens under eighteen without parental consent.

The following week, Larkin had an appointment at her pediatrician's office to receive the meningitis booster vaccines she needed before starting college in a couple of years. After the nurse gave her the vaccinations, Larkin asked if she could ask Dr. Mills a question. The doctor was on vacation, but the nurse offered to have another pediatrician talk to her.

A few minutes later, the exam room door opened. A man stepped in and introduced himself as Dr. Lyons. He was tall with a square jaw and a long, pointed nose offset by large nostrils that flared slightly when his mouth was closed. He wore a checkered short-sleeved shirt, khaki pants, and pristine white tennis shoes. His purple tie was embellished with lion heads wearing gold crowns. He kept one hand on the open door's knob as he asked what he could do for her today.

Lyons? Lions? Larkin thought. She wondered if his choice of tie had some other meaning or was just a coincidence.

She explained to Dr. Lyons that her friend had wanted to get the HPV shot at the health department, but they had recently changed their policies. She asked if there was somewhere else her friend could go.

Without hesitating, he bluntly said her friend should talk to her parents about it.

"They told her 'no' already, but she would still like to get it," Larkin replied.

"Then she'll have to wait until she's eighteen to make those decisions. Let her know she can decrease her risk of getting HPV to zero by abstaining from high-risk activities. Then she won't need to worry about needing the vaccine, right?" He paused and gave Larkin a smile. He briefly took his hand off the doorknob to pull a business card from his front pocket and then handed it to Larkin.

"Have your friend go to this website. I think it would have some useful information for her. For you as well."

Dr. Lyons left the room, and Larkin looked at the card. It was the website for Make the Right Choice, the organization that had spoken to Larkin's seventh-grade class. Under the web address, it read, "Dan Lyons, MD – Medical Director."

Larkin texted Aubrey later.

i asked another doctor where you can get the vaccine
and?
he lowkey slut-shamed you

CHAPTER 12

March 21, 2032
The Tennessean
Tennessee follows lead of other Southern states, bans out-of-state travel for abortions

Spencer called everyone who had just recently been so overjoyed about a new family member to let them know the devastating news. Their parents offered words of comfort and wanted to visit or help in some way, but Spencer declined. He and Larkin needed their privacy.

Larkin was now fourteen weeks pregnant, and she and Spencer had finally accepted that the ultrasound hadn't been wrong. They both knew their baby was going to die, they just didn't know when that time would come. They also knew that no amount of wishing or praying for a different outcome would change their baby's fate.

Dr. Beyer was the maternal-fetal medicine specialist who took over Larkin's care. When he repeated the ultrasound, he showed them where the brain should be—on the screen, that spot was just a dark void. He also told them she was a girl, something Dr. Parrish had not said. Larkin wondered if it had been too early to tell or if Dr. Parrish had been distracted by the unexpected and tragic news she'd had to deliver to a hopeful young couple.

"We're having a girl," Larkin repeated, and for a fleeting moment, she felt happy. It sounded so normal.

"Yes. Females tend to have a higher rate of anencephaly compared to males. About three to four times as high," Dr. Beyer responded.

Larkin closed her eyes. The brief glimpse of normalcy was now gone.

"I'm going to have you meet with a genetic consultant today. They will take a family history to see if there are any genetic risk factors, and they'll discuss the risk of possible recurrence. We would also recommend amniocentesis to look for chromosomal anomalies that may be associated with anencephaly. And we'll need to discuss what to expect during your pregnancy. I'll give you a minute, and we can meet in my office to discuss further."

In his office, Dr. Beyer sat with Larkin and Spencer and showed them illustrations of a baby with anencephaly. He explained that a large portion of their baby's brain, the cerebrum, was missing and is needed for thinking, seeing, hearing, touch, and voluntary movement. He also explained there was no bone on the back of her head.

"Her breathing, heartbeat, and body temperature will still be functional at birth because the brain stem is likely still intact. Most newborns will die within the first few hours or days of life, though about 10 percent may live up to one week. She will die from cardiorespiratory arrest."

"I can't do this," Larkin stated flatly.

"I know it's difficult to hear this, but it's important to be informed."

"No. I can't do *this*. This pregnancy. I can't live with the reality of growing a baby inside of me for five or six more months and then watching her slowly die. I can't."

"I'm sorry, Larkin. It is an incredibly difficult situation."

"It's too difficult. I can't. I want an abortion." She turned to her husband. "I want an abortion. Please. I can't do this."

Spencer looked at her helplessly as he saw the hurt and desperation in her eyes.

"I'm sorry, Larkin. That isn't an option in this state," Dr. Beyer replied.

"Yes, I know. I'll go out of state. Where can I go? Atlanta? Somewhere in the Northeast? I'll go anywhere. Please just tell me where."

"It's illegal to travel out of state for an abortion. You could have at one time, but not now. The legislation passed in the spring. If you try to do that, the state you went to would have to refuse you or they would be breaking the law. You would also be breaking the law. There will likely be more legislation passed soon. If that happens, I would have to report you to a database if I thought you might seek an abortion."

"You're telling me I have no choice? That I have to carry this baby to term?"

"Yes."

"Who decided that? Who decided that for me? For Spencer? For my baby? Is this what you would want for your wife? Your daughter? Is this what you want for your patients?" Larkin said, her voice rising.

"What I would want has no bearing on this. It's the law."

"If I lived in another state, I could have an abortion?"

"Yes. Over half the states still allow it in this case."

"I'm just trying to make sure I understand this. I am pregnant with a baby who has 0 percent chance of survival, and I am being forced by the legal system to carry this baby to term. Is that what you are telling me?"

"Yes." Dr. Beyer looked away from her and stroked his chin. He cleared his throat and continued. "Now, we need to talk about potential complications for you during the pregnancy. Many women will experience polyhydramnios—"

"I can't talk about this anymore right now, Dr. Beyer," Larkin interrupted. "I need to go." She stood up to leave.

"Understandable, Larkin. We can discuss more next time."

Larkin grabbed Spencer's hand. They walked out of Dr. Beyer's office and into a waiting room full of expectant mothers. Spencer stopped by the receptionist's window to schedule a follow-up appointment with Dr. Beyer and to reschedule the visit with the geneticist. Larkin scanned the waiting room crowd and wondered if any of the other women had been told they were also carrying a baby that was going to die. Searching their faces to see if she could tell, she tried to recognize any communal pain.

In the car, she told Spencer again that she couldn't do this.

"I'm not strong enough. I can't handle this. I can't go to bed every night praying for a miscarriage that may never happen; I don't *want* to pray for that. But I can't handle the alternative."

"I'm so, so sorry. It's not fair—it's not right. If I could somehow help you fix this, I would."

"Can you please take me home? Susan knew I had an appointment this morning, but I didn't tell her what it was for. I'll text her to let her know I'm not feeling well."

"Of course. Do you want me to stay with you?"

"No, thank you. I promise I'll be okay. I know you need to go to work."

Spencer took Larkin home and made her a cup of hot tea. He placed it on the nightstand beside her and helped get her comfortable in bed.

"I'll be back in a few hours, okay?" he said as he kissed her head and pulled the comforter up for her.

She nodded and rolled over in silence.

CHAPTER 13

Spencer had decided to give his two weeks' notice to Mr. Montgomery today. He pulled into the insurance agency's parking lot and turned off his car. He hadn't found another job, but he didn't need to anymore. There was no need to save up for a baby who didn't have a future. He held the steering wheel tightly as he started to weep.

He wiped his tears with his sleeve and looked at the building. Employees had taken down the campaign posters and replaced them with congratulatory banners. Mr. Montgomery had won the election and would be sworn in to the US Senate in January. The protesters who'd posted the video had achieved nothing other than a few days of social media outrage with angry emojis and comments for and against, but then it had been forgotten. Jack Montgomery had won by a landslide against his Democratic opponent, as had traditionally and predictably happened in their state for years.

Spencer and Larkin hadn't voted. They hadn't even remembered when it was Election Day. They had been too consumed with shock and grief to think of much beyond the pregnancy.

When Spencer walked into the agency, his boss was sitting in his office and shuffling through some papers. Spencer knocked on the frame of the open door and asked if he had a minute to talk.

"Why, sure, Spencer, come on in! Just organizing some things before my new gig starts in January. I'm looking forward to changing some things in this country. Keep us on the right track, you know?"

Spencer stayed in the doorframe. He said, "Not really, no. But what I wanted to talk to you about is my job. I'd like to put in my two weeks' notice."

"Oh, my. Did you find something better?"

"No, sir."

"Well, I'm sorry to hear that, Spencer. I think you have great potential to be an insurance agent, and I could really use you as I travel back and forth between here and DC. I was even planning to give you a raise. Figured you could use the extra income for that little one you have coming."

"There won't be a little one."

"Oh, son. Did she miscarry? That's just terrible."

"No, no . . . it's worse than that. The baby has a birth defect that's not survivable, but she may not die until after she's born." As the words came out of his mouth, Spencer hung his head. He couldn't believe it was his reality. Larkin's reality.

"Well, now. Yes, that is a tragedy. I'll be praying for strength for you and Larkin."

Spencer felt anger building up inside of him. He looked down at the floor. "Respectfully, we don't want or need your prayers."

"C'mon, now. I know this must be difficult, but everyone can use a prayer, Spencer. The power of prayer means salvation and healing. 'And all things, whatsoever you shall ask in prayer, believing, you shall receive.'"

Spencer looked at Jack with disbelief. "Then pray for my wife to be able to get an abortion," he said. "That's what she needs to heal."

"You know I can't do that—I can't pray for a sin to be committed. I know you're in pain, Larkin's in pain, but this is all part of God's plan. You may not understand His plan, but you need to have faith in Him and His will."

"Is it His will or your will, Jack? My wife is a living, breathing, loving, kind, wonderful human here on this earth who isn't allowed to decide what is best for her physical and mental health. And after she is forced to give birth . . . forced . . . by people like you . . . I don't know when or if she will ever be ready to have another baby. And now you want to take away birth control, too. Why? It's cruel. And it's none of your business."

"Well, we will have to disagree then. Birth control is used to abort babies. I know you know that. You're a smart college boy, now, aren't you? I will never support that. And if God blesses you and Larkin with another baby someday, you should be thankful for that."

"I think your self-righteousness has killed your humanity."

"My 'self-righteousness,' as you say, keeps babies like yours from being killed."

Spencer clenched his fists. He wanted to punch his boss in the face. Over and over and over again. If he started, he didn't know if he would ever be able to stop. He wanted him to hurt like Larkin was hurting, but he knew the physical pain he could inflict on Jack wouldn't compare to what she was feeling. He said nothing more and walked out. He just wanted to be home with his wife.

CHAPTER 14

Larkin had bought a lot of long, loose shirts and pants with elastic waistbands, but she was having trouble hiding her pregnancy anymore. She was now eighteen weeks pregnant, and the telltale bump was becoming more obvious. Her breasts were getting bigger. Her feet were starting to swell if she stood for too long.

She was in her cubicle working on her part of a grant for Dr. Davis when Susan came by. Larkin rolled her chair as close to her desk as she could to camouflage her belly.

"Larkin, would you like to come to lunch with me? It's been a long time. I thought we could catch up."

Larkin agreed, and Susan drove them to a restaurant nearby. As they were waiting by the hostess stand, the young hostess looked Larkin up and down and brightly exclaimed, "Oh, congratulations, Mommy! Please sit, sit, sit! We will get you a table as soon as we can."

Larkin hastily sat down on a bench without saying a word to Susan. She placed her purse on her lap. Susan sat beside her in polite silence, pretending not to have heard the hostess.

Once they were seated at their table, Susan said kindly, "Larkin . . . I want you to know it's okay. I know you're pregnant. We all know you're pregnant."

Larkin ran her thumb and forefinger along the side of her water glass, focusing on the condensation. She couldn't get any words out.

"No one ever wants to tell me they're pregnant since all my miscarriages," Susan said. "I promise, I am happy for you. I've known for a while now with your appointments and missed work. I figured you must be having a lot of morning sickness. And I would really love to have a baby shower for you. This is something to be celebrated, okay? Don't worry about me. It used to bother me. Now, I would be envious if you got a new kitten," Susan said, smiling.

"Oh, Susan. That's not why I haven't said anything."

Larkin started to say more but paused when the waiter dropped off an appetizer. She sat back, clasped her hands together on the table, and wondered how to tell Susan about her baby's birth defect. Then the words started pouring out. She told her how she'd found out she was pregnant when she was at work—that was the day she didn't feel well—and Susan took her to Dr. Davis's office for the first time. She told her about the ultrasound and how she and Spencer had cried. She told her about all she had been reading online and in the literature from the doctor's office. She told her about asking Abdullah about abortion. She told her how she'd decided what she wanted to do but was told she couldn't.

And she told Susan she had been hiding the pregnancy because she didn't want to answer the same questions again and again, knowing that everyone would be so happy for her and she'd have to tell them they shouldn't be.

She told her all of this while never taking her eyes off of the glass in front of her, watching the drops of water slowly run down the side of the glass and spread on the table. She felt as though she could collapse into a puddle as well and wished a waiter could just wipe her up and toss her away.

"Oh, my God. I am so sorry. I had no idea," Susan said. She reached for Larkin's hands and held them in hers.

"I didn't want you to have any idea," Larkin said. "I knew I couldn't hide it forever, though."

"Do you want me to tell anyone at work so you don't have to? Would you rather tell them?"

"No, please. That would be great if you could tell Abdullah, Alondra, and Kai. And please tell Dr. Davis for me."

"Of course, dear. And if Spencer can't take you for an appointment or you just need someone to talk to, please let me know. Or if you need any time off from work."

"Thank you so much. I will," Larkin replied as she dabbed tears from her eyes with a napkin.

"And the worst part. Lately . . ." Larkin exhaled and looked at Susan as she continued to speak. "The worst part is that she's kicking now. I can feel her. It's a literal punch to my gut every single time it happens."

As Susan regarded her with sorrow, Larkin knew she looked frail and broken and scared. Dr. Beyer had put her on Zoloft. She hadn't been sleeping well, and she made herself eat for the baby. Every minute of her life was consumed with dread as she waited for the day her baby would be born, and now she was no longer able to hide her pain or her pregnancy.

She was relieved that she had told Susan, and she was thankful that Susan would tell everyone else. She knew her simple presence would make others uncomfortable because they wouldn't know what to say. She was prepared for awkward moments in the lab, along with more looks of pity and compassion, but it would be a safe zone compared to being out in public.

Pregnancy was always an easy conversation starter. No matter where Larkin went, and as hard as she tried not to make eye contact, strangers (overwhelmingly, well-meaning older women) would approach her and congratulate her. They would ask when she was due, ask if she was having a boy or a girl, and ask what name she had chosen. They also offered advice on how to induce labor: drink red raspberry leaf tea, have sex near your due date, have your husband stimulate your nipples.

They sometimes overshared details of their own pregnancy horror stories. She was amazed at how much interest others showed in her pregnancy. She felt like pregnancy was a joyful club and she was only an honorary member. But the intrusions never made Larkin angry—she knew they wanted to help, and she knew they wanted to share in what they assumed was a happy time in her life.

Without fail, she would politely respond, "May 22. A girl. We haven't picked a name yet. Thank you for the advice."

Spencer and Larkin hadn't picked a name yet, but they knew she deserved to be named, and it was time. She needed to be more than just "the baby" or "she" or "her." They struggled to decide the best way to honor her and the best way to remember her after.

After.

After she was gone.

They decided to name her after how they'd felt when they first saw her heart beating—the excitement they'd felt when they were anticipating good news and the brief period of time when they were planning for a much different "after."

They agreed on Maeve.

CHAPTER 15

Maeve: *Irish. Cause of great joy.*

Just after the winter holidays, the young couple met with the geneticist. Larkin had an amniocentesis and more ultrasounds. There was no family history of neural tube defects. There were no chromosomal anomalies identified. They were told there was a one in fifty chance that this could happen again, and they would never know for certain why it happened.

When Larkin was about twenty-eight weeks pregnant, they met with a neonatal palliative care team. Dr. Beyer and the attending physician of the neonatal intensive care unit, along with a NICU charge nurse, a chaplain, and a social worker, gathered in a conference room at the hospital where Larkin would deliver. Dr. Beyer said that if Larkin didn't go into labor on her own, he recommended that she be induced at thirty-nine weeks gestation. Dr. Parrish would complete her obstetric care and be there for the delivery. Larkin and Spencer were told what to expect that day. They were asked who they wanted to be present during and after the delivery and which funeral home they would prefer to handle the arrangements. The nurse jotted down their wishes.

Larkin and Spencer asked about donating Maeve's organs for transplantation, as they had heard parents of anencephalic babies had done this in the past. They hoped it would help them in the grieving process knowing that her short life had helped others live longer.

"Unfortunately, no." Dr. Beyer explained that after abortion had been completely banned in the state and out-of-state travel for abortion had also been made illegal, hospital ethics boards in Tennessee had put a hold on any organ donations from neonates with lethal anomalies.

Dr. Beyer clarified, "An ethics committee would need to review the ramifications of this new law to ensure that a mother's decision to donate her baby's organs is made freely, without coercion or undue pressure resulting from her inability to access abortion. Additionally, the committee needs to assess whether the law creates an implicit incentive for states to enforce birth in cases of lethal fetal anomalies to increase organ availability."

"But we *are* making this decision freely. Isn't that enough?" Larkin implored.

Spencer added, "We would like some good to come of all this. It would help us to know Maeve helped other babies. That there was some purpose to her death. Right now, we can't make sense of it."

Dr. Beyer regarded Larkin and Spencer with quiet understanding and a mournful gaze.

The social worker chimed in to shatter the uncomfortable pause, "We are so sorry, but our hands are tied. We are going to need to move on. We have a lot to discuss."

Larkin stared down at Spencer's hand as he held it in hers. She placed her other hand on her belly as she felt Maeve shift inside of her. Maeve's soft nudge felt like an acknowledgement that she knew her mom was trying her best.

The team explained what Larkin and Spencer should expect as best as they could foresee. They made sure to refer to Maeve by name as they provided the details. Larkin and Spencer would have a private room in the NICU after the delivery. They could both stay there and hold Maeve before she died, if she wasn't stillborn. A nurse would check on them periodically but would otherwise give them time alone. Maeve would be on a monitor to check her heart rate and breathing, but there would be no interventions when she took her last breaths. They expected her breathing to slow at first, and then her heart would stop beating. She might have some gasping breaths—agonal respirations—that might last for several minutes, and then she would be gone. They didn't know if she would live for minutes, hours, or days.

Larkin focused on the phrase "agonal respirations" and thought of agony, agonizing, anguish.

The conversation was surreal. It seemed more fitting for a family preparing for the death of their ninety-year-old patriarch who was on hospice care with a terminal cancer diagnosis, not a newborn baby. A baby whose sole experience in this world would be a womb and then a hospital room.

It seemed as if Maeve wanted to stay safe inside of her mother for as long as she could, as though she knew what her fate would be upon birth. After Dr. Parrish checked Larkin at thirty-eight weeks, she scheduled the induction for the following week. Larkin had developed worsening polyhydramnios—a large buildup of amniotic fluid—which was common in mothers of anencephalic babies. She was having difficulty breathing because of the extra fluid, and the swelling in her legs was getting worse. She'd had a procedure to drain the excess fluid a couple of weeks ago, but it had already reaccumulated. Walking up just a few stairs made her short of breath.

Larkin's heart raced at the thought of a scheduled induction date. She'd known that the day was inevitable, but now an actual date had been chosen for Maeve. A date that once had been just another number on a calendar would now and forever be a painful anniversary memorializing a tragic loss.

The induction was scheduled to start in the evening of Larkin's thirty-ninth week. Maeve's parents arrived at the admitting desk near the hospital entrance with their overnight bags. The clerk took their insurance card and looked at their belongings. She reminded them to bring a car seat for discharge.

"You know you can't leave the hospital without a car seat for your baby," she said as she sorted through paperwork, stapling and clipping. "A lot of new parents forget. So many things to remember about taking care of a new little life, right?" She placed a plastic armband on Larkin's wrist and gave Spencer a visitor's tag.

Spencer nodded and thanked her. Larkin thought, *She's just being kind. She doesn't know.*

They took the elevator to the hospital's third floor and walked to the labor and delivery unit. As they walked across the freshly buffed floor to the busy front desk, the intercom overhead started playing a music box version of "Brahms' Lullaby," announcing the recent delivery of a newborn. The lady seated behind the counter smiled at Larkin and Spencer and said energetically, "Welcome! You'll be hearing that music for your baby soon enough!"

Larkin again forced a smile as she thought, *She doesn't know.*

The receptionist asked to see Larkin's armband and pulled up the "expect sheet" on the computer, which would have a summary of their birth plan and the name of their obstetrician. She read the first line in all capital letters and immediately apologized.

"I am so sorry. I'll get the charge nurse," she said quietly as she got up and walked briskly to a nearby office.

The charge nurse came to the front desk right away. She was the same nurse who had been in the care team meeting a couple of months ago. She ushered the couple to a labor and delivery room, another nurse following behind them.

"Hello again. Please, have a seat. I sincerely apologize for what just happened. We had told everyone you were coming today, but she didn't realize right away that it was you."

"It's really okay," Spencer said.

Larkin echoed his words. "Hopefully this kind of delivery doesn't happen often."

"No, it doesn't, but it's getting more common. Thank you both for understanding." She turned to the nurse behind her and said, "This is Angela. She'll be taking care of you during her shift. She will take very good care of you both." She excused herself to let the RN take over.

Angela looked to be in her early thirties with curly, bright red hair and stylish tortoiseshell glasses. She was a travel nurse from Texas who was working at the hospital on a six-month contract. She asked Larkin when she'd last had anything to eat or drink and if she had any allergies. Angela then told Larkin to change into a gown so she could check her cervix and start her IV.

When Angela came back into the room, Spencer and Larkin heard the lullaby playing overhead as she opened the door.

"Sounds like it's been a busy day for deliveries," Spencer commented.

"Yes. It must have been the heat wave last summer. Everyone stayed indoors with nothing else to do, I guess," she quipped.

Angela tied a tourniquet around Larkin's upper left arm and then cleaned the crook of her elbow with an alcohol wipe. She straightened Larkin's arm and used her gloved index finger to feel for the spongy vein before inserting a needle. A flash of blood passed through the cannula, and Angela advanced it forward.

"Alright! First try! That never gets old," Angela exclaimed as she flushed the IV with saline, taped it in place, and hooked it up to the rest of the IV apparatus. "We are going to start you on Cytotec first. That will get your cervix ready before we start your Pitocin, which will get your contractions going."

Angela took a gloved hand, checked Larkin's cervix, and placed the Cytotec inside her vagina.

"My mom used to sing me that lullaby in German when I was little," Larkin said as Angela finished the cervical exam and adjusted the IV pole.

"Mine, too! We still have family in Stuttgart, and my grandparents live in New Braunfels, Texas, where a lot of Germans settled."

"We have relatives there and in Nuremberg," Larkin replied.

"*Kleine welt.*" Angela grinned and put a warm blanket on Larkin. "Tonight will probably be pretty boring for you. We just need time to get your cervix prepared for delivery. I'll be checking on you every so often, usually right about the time when you have just fallen asleep." She laughed. "Push this red button if you need me," Angela said as she handed Larkin a device that hung on the side of the bed.

Spencer had brought a small speaker to the hospital. He turned it on and played some music from Larkin's playlist. He sat beside her and held her hand. "Hey. I know this is a dumb question, but how are you feeling?"

"Not dumb. I'm sad. Anxious. Happy we're together."

"Same," Spencer said as he brushed her hair out of her face. He set up her bedside table with her hand lotion, lip balm, and phone charger. Then he settled into the recliner next to her with a pillow and blanket. They both slept off and on through the night, waking when Angela came in to check Larkin's vital signs and cervix.

The next morning, Angela came in to tell them goodbye at the end of her shift and introduced them to the nurse who would be taking over for the day. Allina looked to be younger than Angela and was just as friendly. She wore a blue lanyard with bichon frise dogs all over it and a gold necklace with a photo of a little boy in a small heart frame. She told them she was fluent in English, Spanish, and Tagalog and had worked in the labor and delivery unit for three years.

Angela expected that Larkin would still be there when she came back for her evening shift as primips take longer to induce.

"Primips?" Spencer asked.

"Yes, first pregnancies. Inductions can take two to three days sometimes. Maeve is on the smaller side, so it may take less time," Angela explained.

The thought of waiting that long to deliver was bittersweet to Larkin. She would be able to keep Maeve inside her longer, but that would only delay the inevitable. Larkin wasn't sure what she wanted, but it didn't really matter—the Cytotec would decide for her.

After twenty-two hours since Larkin arrived, Allina told her that her cervix was ready to start the Pitocin, and she changed out the IV fluids for medicine. "The anesthesiologist will be in to start your epidural once you're about four to five centimeters dilated," Allina told Larkin.

Spencer left for a quick trip to a nearby fast-food restaurant to get her a cup of her favorite crushed ice.

Since being admitted the night before, Larkin had been getting texts from family members, friends, and coworkers who were thinking of her and Spencer. She replied with simple heart emojis and thank-yous. As she looked out her hospital window, she could see the sun was setting and the sky was a beautiful array of pastels.

The first contraction came, and Larkin's gaze shifted from the window to the monitor next to her. It didn't hurt like she had expected it to. It felt like a quick jolt and squeeze to her abdomen, and she saw the spike appear on the monitor as it happened, but it wasn't bad at all. She hoped Spencer would get back before it got worse.

She texted Aubrey: *hey you*

hey!!!!!!! i have been thinking about you a lot but i didn't want to bother you. i love you and spencer and i am sending you soooooo many hugs and soooooo much love.

Larkin felt another quick jolt and replied, *thank you friend. i am just starting to contract.*

have they checked your cervix lately? got the epidural yet? you are getting an epidural right?

yes no and hell yes

good. i want you to be comfortable ok? and don't let some resident do your epidural. i know it's how we learn but i don't want anyone practicing on you

Larkin smiled as she texted: *good advice. i won't*

and i know you don't want anyone there besides spencer but i wish i could be with you

i know you do. thank you for understanding

when you are feeling up to it, come visit. or i can come there ok?

of course

kisses

Larkin hesitated to reply, then typed, *i'm really scared*

want me to call?

no. i just wanted to know you are there.

always

Spencer walked in with Larkin's big cup of ice and kissed her on her head. Allina came in behind him and checked her cervix again.

"You're about three centimeters, Larkin," Allina announced as she removed her gloves. "You'll probably be ready for your epidural in another hour or so."

The contractions were starting to feel stronger, but Larkin was still surprised at how mild the pain was. She wondered if her emotional pain was blunting her physical pain. Or maybe her body knew she couldn't handle both and was extending her a simple kindness.

Shortly after Allina left, the anesthesiologist had her sign the consent for the epidural and explained the procedure. She asked him if he was a resident or a fully trained doctor. He grinned and asked if she knew someone in medical school.

"Yes, why?" Larkin asked.

"Because medical students never want other students or residents practicing on the people they love." He chuckled and promised he had done thousands of epidurals. He also said he was glad she had a good friend watching out for her.

Once Larkin was about four centimeters dilated, the anesthesiologist came back. He had her sit up on the bed as he sat behind her. She felt something cold and wet on her back as he explained that he was sterilizing the area. He told her she would feel a pinch to her lower back while he injected numbing medication. Then he placed the epidural.

"You're a champ, Larkin. All done," the anesthesiologist told her. "The pain medication should start working in about fifteen minutes or so."

It was becoming more and more real that she was having her baby today. She was sure there had to be other women on the same floor experiencing the same things: the contractions, the cervical checks, the epidural placement. But she was sure they were excited and had friends and family with them and in the waiting room. As she watched her contractions becoming more frequent on the monitor, Larkin wondered if they would play the lullaby announcement for Maeve.

Angela took over for Allina as the evening staff started arriving.

"Back again!" Angela exclaimed. "Allina told me you have been progressing well. I'll be back to check you again later. There's going to be a full moon tonight, so we can expect a lot more babies, like yesterday. Maybe even more. Some nurses say it's just a myth, but I'm a believer. Those same nurses always make sure to ask for the night off every full moon, though," she said, rolling her eyes. Larkin could tell she was only pretending to be irritated.

Spencer was in the chair beside her, updating family members via text. Larkin looked down at her pregnant belly and held it. She would rather stay like this forever than give birth.

Angela came in again and checked her at about one in the morning. "You're getting very close, Larkin. Dr. Parrish has been calling to check on you. I'll let her know when to come."

Spencer had dozed off. Larkin gently grabbed his arm to wake him. "It's almost time," she said.

He leaned over and kissed her hand, her arm, and her cheeks. "I love you more than anything, Larky Lark."

"I love you, too, Spence."

Angela stopped in for one more cervical check. "It's time to call Dr. Parrish," she said.

It's time, Larkin thought. *I'm not ready. I'll never be ready.* When she felt a wave of panic, she tried to focus on breathing slowly.

Dr. Parrish came in, greeted them both, and right away gowned and gloved for the delivery. Angela helped Larkin bend her legs and put her knees near her shoulders. She moved her closer to Dr. Parrish, who was adjusting a sterile drape. Dr. Parrish grabbed an instrument—it looked like a long crochet hook—and shortly afterward, there was a large gush of water that seemed to go on forever. Another nurse came in to help hold Larkin's legs.

As the next contraction came, Dr. Parrish told Larkin to push like she was having a bowel movement. Angela told her to tuck her chin to her chest and start pushing hard while she breathed through her mouth. Larkin repeated this as several more contractions came, with Spencer encouraging her and wiping sweat from her forehead with a cool washcloth.

Larkin heard the NICU team come into the room and the sounds they made while getting their supplies ready. She heard plastic packaging being opened, metal objects being set down, and instructions being given as to who would bring the baby to the warmer and who would assign the Apgar scores. She also heard the incubator being rolled next to the warmer. While she was resting after the last contraction, she saw the warming bed had been turned on, the light glowing on a blanket and stethoscope below. The team stood there in blue gowns, wearing masks and gloves and surgical caps with only their eyes visible, waiting for Maeve to arrive. She wondered how often they came to a delivery like this, and if it got easier for them each time. She also wondered if staying detached was an innate skill or if it was learned with time.

"Okay, Larkin, one more hard push," Dr. Parrish said. "Right now. You can do this. Breathe through your mouth and push, push, push, push!"

"You can do this, Larkin," Spencer said encouragingly.

I can. I can. I don't want to. I have to. I'm sorry, Maeve, I'm sorry, she thought.

"Push, push, push!" Angela repeated.

"Good job! Here she comes!"

"One more big push, Larkin!"

She pushed as hard as she could and then heard Dr. Parrish yell, "Good job. She's here!" The doctor grabbed a blue bulb syringe and suctioned Maeve's mouth and nose.

Larkin and Spencer heard a weak, wet cry. They got a quick glimpse of her, bloody and purple, as Dr. Parrish handed her to the neonatology team. They wouldn't resuscitate her if she stopped breathing, but they were there in part because it was a teaching hospital and most of the residents had not seen an anencephalic baby before.. As they dried and suctioned her further, Maeve didn't cry anymore. Larkin and Spencer strained to see past the doctors and nurses who huddled around their newborn and murmured about "respiratory effort" and "muscle tone."

After a few more minutes, the neonatology team quietly filed out of the room, and Angela gently placed Maeve skin to skin on Larkin's chest. On Maeve's head was a small, white knitted cap that had been made by a hospital volunteer. Larkin was thankful for this, and she was sure Spencer was, too. They wanted to see the rest of Maeve—not her defect. They had seen enough babies on the internet that they knew what to expect. They didn't want that to be part of their memory bank for this day.

Larkin and Spencer looked at every inch of her tiny body below the little beanie and slowly took her in. She had perfect fingers and toes. One hand was wrapped around Spencer's finger. They knew it was simply a reflex, but it still made them smile. Maeve's back felt smooth and warm as her mother rubbed her hand against it. Larkin could feel her daughter's chest rise on hers, along with the fast beating of her heart. Her mouth and nose were perfect. Her eyes were closed, a little puffy and swollen. She looked like any other baby as long as the cap covered her head.

After Dr. Parrish sewed up a small tear in Larkin's vagina, Larkin was moved to a wheelchair with Maeve still on her chest. Spencer gathered up their things, and Angela pushed them to their room in the NICU. The room was called the Tranquility Room, and it had soft lighting and a queen bed. Watercolor paintings of nature scenes hung from the walls. Two large recliners and a coffee table were across from the bed. Larkin wondered how many parents before her had said their goodbyes in this room.

Angela got Larkin settled into bed, and their neonatology nurse, Betty, came in and introduced herself. Betty had over forty years of experience and was confident and motherly. Her silver hair was held back in a tight bun. During her career, she had taken care of at least a dozen other anencephalic babies at all different stages. Some were stillborn. Some had lived only a few minutes. One had lived three weeks—her mother had been barely out of high school and had left the hospital with her boyfriend, abandoning her baby girl when she was less than 24 hours old. No family members had come to see her, and the Department of Children's Services had made arrangements for her body when she'd died.

Betty put Maeve on a monitor and told Spencer and Larkin she would be just outside the door if they needed anything. When the monitor came on, they could hear the fast, steady beating of Maeve's heart.

Angela said goodbye and thanked them for letting her help take care of Maeve. She promised she would have them play the lullaby for Maeve before she left.

Spencer lay in the bed next to Larkin. She tried to offer Maeve her breast, but Maeve didn't attempt to latch or seem interested, and Larkin called for Betty to help. Betty showed her how to hand-express colostrum from her breast, and they gave Maeve small amounts in a syringe, but she took very little.

Larkin and Spencer were both exhausted but too anxious to go to sleep. They knew the monitor was on and Betty was just outside the door, but it did not help them relax. The room that had been designed to offer tranquility had failed.

Larkin looked at the baby she and Spencer had made, however imperfectly, now sleeping soundly on her chest. The lullaby started to play overhead for Maeve, just as Angela had promised. Larkin knew Maeve couldn't hear her voice, but she wanted to sing for her in the only German she knew, the lullaby her mother had sung for her:

Guten Abend, gut' Nacht,
mit Rosen bedacht,
mit Näglein besteckt,
schlupf' unter die Deck':
Morgen früh, wenn Gott will,
wirst du wieder geweckt,
morgen früh, wenn Gott will,
wirst du wieder geweckt.

Guten Abend, gut' Nacht,
von Englein bewacht,
die zeigen im Traum
dir Christkindleins Baum:
Schlaf nun selig und süß.
schlau im Traum's Paradies,
schlaf nun selig und süß.
schlau im Traum's Paradies.

Larkin kissed Maeve's cheek and hoped that maybe she could dream, despite what the doctors had said about her level of awareness and what she knew logically to be true. She hoped after this life, there would be a beautiful life ahead of her in a place where she was whole and could live the life that had been denied to her.

The new parents spent their time with Maeve telling her how much they loved her and softly singing their favorite songs to her. The beeping on the monitor suddenly started to slow. The number that had been wavering between 140 and 160 dropped to 78, then 54, then 42. Betty came in and turned off the monitor, as she'd been instructed by the neonatologist. She told Spencer and Larkin that Maeve's heart was shutting down.

Larkin felt her own heart beating faster and faster, rising up as if it could jump out of her throat. She felt like she could barely breathe. Her hands tingled with a feeling of pins and needles.

Betty asked if Larkin wanted her to stay with them or get the doctor. Larkin shook her head quickly. She just wanted it to be her, Spencer, and Maeve. Spencer was a quiet but steady presence. He didn't cry. He didn't speak. But she felt his arms around her, holding her tight, kissing the top of her head.

They swaddled Maeve in a hospital blanket printed with pastel ducklings and sat up in bed, taking turns holding her. After a few minutes, Maeve started to gasp like a fish out of water. Her mouth opened and closed like a goldfish that had jumped out of its bowl. Her sweet, perfect face turned blue. She seemed hungry for oxygen but at the same time was drowning in air she couldn't breathe.

Although Spencer and Larkin had been told that this would happen, it was more agonizing to watch than they'd expected. The feelings of helplessness that washed over them were unbearable.

Larkin could only weep and whisper into Maeve's knitted cap, "I'm sorry. I'm so sorry. I'm sorry."

After three hours and twenty-seven minutes in this world, Maeve was gone.

CHAPTER 16

The old Lie: Dulce et Decorum est . . .
—Wilfred Owen, poet

Betty came in and listened to Maeve's heart and lungs, then texted the neonatologist on call. The neonatologist listened again to Maeve's quiet, unmoving chest and officially pronounced the time of death.

Betty brought in a small crib for Maeve. It had a special cooling mattress inside. The care team had told Larkin and Spencer about this months ago. It would keep Maeve's body maintained for longer so they could spend more time with her. Larkin and Spencer called their parents so they could come to the hospital to meet and then say goodbye to their only grandchild.

Larkin and Spencer asked Betty to take Maeve for what would be her first and last bath. She left for a bit and came back with Maeve dressed in a tiny white gown with eyelet lace trim and a matching soft white hat with a small bow on the side. It looked like a dress for a child's baby doll, and Betty told them it was. The NICU nurses and volunteers kept a donated supply of little clothes like these for times like this.

The nursing staff had made a remembrance card with Maeve's hand- and footprints. Betty also gave them a lock of Maeve's hair, tied with a pink ribbon. Spencer and Larkin had noticed a little bit of dark hair peeking out from under her hat—it looked just like Spencer's. Betty asked if they would like for her to take pictures of them holding Maeve. They thanked her for offering and agreed.

After Betty took the pictures with Spencer's phone, Larkin said quietly to her, "After our families visit, I don't remember what we do next."

Betty explained that they could take Maeve home for a little while and then bring her back if they wanted. They would provide them with a Moses basket and the cooling mattress if that's what they wanted to do. Or the funeral director could bring Maeve to their house. Otherwise, if they preferred, Maeve could go directly to the funeral home and they could arrange to have her buried or cremated.

Larkin had forgotten they had been told months ago that they were able to take Maeve home before she went to the funeral home. Larkin could carry her in her arms while Spencer drove. Betty told them the hospital would provide them with a letter to give to a police officer if they got pulled over, and the NICU would alert the police before they left the hospital. The thought of explaining to law enforcement why their baby was not in a car seat and then having to provide a letter explaining the circumstances filled Larkin with dread. They decided to have the funeral director take her from the hospital and have her cremated.

"There are no wrong decisions," Betty said. "We want you both to do whatever makes you comfortable. You're her parents. It's your choice, okay?"

Larkin nodded and thought, *My choice. After all these months of carrying her. After all this pain and worry. After watching Maeve gasp, watching her turn blue, watching her die. Now I have a choice.* It provided her little comfort.

Spencer and Larkin showered and dressed, preparing for their parents' arrival. Larkin looked at herself when she stepped out of the shower. Her face and legs were still puffy and swollen. Her belly still looked very pregnant. Her breasts were starting to engorge with milk that wouldn't be used to nourish her baby. She looked so much older now than her twenty-three years, and she felt like a completely different person.

It was, of course, a somber moment when their parents arrived with flowers that would wilt and favorite foods that would go uneaten. They took turns holding Maeve and commenting about how she had Spencer's hair and big feet but Larkin's nose. Spencer and Larkin told them how kind everyone had been and showed them the memorial items the staff had created.

Larkin told her mother that she had sung the German lullaby for Maeve, but they didn't tell the grandparents the details of her death. They wanted to spare them that pain—and spare themselves the pain of reliving those moments. To the grandparents, it all seemed rather peaceful and lovely with Maeve in her eyelet dress and permanent slumber, perhaps dreaming of the paradise mentioned in the lullaby lyrics.

After several hours of visiting, their parents left to stay in hotels near Larkin and Spencer's home. They planned to stay for a few days or longer and help in whatever ways they were needed. After the grandparents gave kisses to Maeve and hugs to Spencer and Larkin, the bereaved young parents were alone again.

Larkin was holding Maeve in her arms, the cooling mattress beneath her, when Spencer asked, "Larkin, are you ready for us to call the funeral director?"

"Yes, I think so," she replied.

"We can wait longer if you want. Whenever you are ready."

"I'm ready."

Betty made the call and gave Spencer and Larkin time to say their goodbyes. They rubbed Maeve's cheeks, which now looked bruised. Her lips were getting darker, and her skin was starting to peel.

Betty came back after making the phone call. She asked if they would like her to take Maeve to the hospital morgue on the basement floor or if they would prefer to take her. Larkin asked Spencer if he would.

Spencer wrapped Maeve in her blanket and kissed Larkin. She watched him as he walked out the door. His head and shoulders drooped, carrying a weight much heavier than the six pounds, five ounces in his arms.

Larkin sat in the chair with the empty crib next to her. She was alone in an empty room. Her body felt empty not carrying Maeve anymore. Her heart felt empty of both blood and emotion. She knew she needed help. Her husband had been unfailingly supportive and her family had been wonderful, but they were also grieving.

Spencer returned from the morgue. They gathered their things, thanked Betty and the staff, and walked out of the hospital, leaving Maeve behind.

CHAPTER 17

Flowers, plants, and cards from family members, Aubrey, Susan, Dr. Davis, Spencer's professors, and others filled the den. The refrigerator and freezer were packed with meals from neighbors. After a few days of visiting, their parents left when Spencer and Larkin reassured them that they were going to be okay.

They had decided not to hold a memorial service. Spencer picked up Maeve's cremains a week after Larkin was released from the hospital. Her ashes had been placed in a tiny silver box with her name and birthdate inscribed on the top. They placed the box on their mantel next to a photo that Betty had taken of Larkin and Spencer holding Maeve, wearing her tiny dress, in those precious few hours they spent with her.

Spencer went back to school the following week to continue in his master's program. He told Larkin he needed to get back into a routine and stay busy. Long before Maeve was born, they had talked many times about how they would grieve differently, and they both understood and respected those differences. Larkin would need more time before she went back to work, and Dr. Davis had kindly told her not to come back to the lab until she felt she was ready. She used the time to visit her parents in her hometown a few hours away and to meet with Aubrey, who was in medical school nearby.

When she arrived at her childhood home, Larkin let herself into the house, went upstairs to her old room, and collapsed in her bed with its wrought iron frame, burying herself in a soft comforter with a mandala print and a sea of plush pillows. Small fairy lights outlined the window above her bed. She hadn't slept well in months, but the comfort and familiarity of her old room allowed her some much-needed rest. As she drifted to sleep, she thought about how her room hadn't changed in the five years since she'd graduated from high school, yet her life was now unrecognizable.

She woke up the next morning feeling groggy even though she had slept for hours. She was still wearing yesterday's clothes as she made her way downstairs, following the smell of coffee, and joined her mom for breakfast.

Although her mother fixed her a plate of eggs and bacon, Larkin only sipped a cup of black coffee. "I just feel so lost, Mom," she said. "I don't know how I am going to be able to get up every day and function and try to be productive. And I am so sorry you and Dad didn't get to be grandparents." Tears fell on the untouched plate of food. "I knew how excited you were to find out I was pregnant."

Her mom reached over and put her hand on hers.

"Larkin, we didn't give birth to you with some great plan that you would give us grandchildren someday. Of course, we were thrilled when you first told us, but we aren't grieving over not being grandparents. We're grieving your loss . . . our child's loss . . . and the loss of Maeve. Nothing more."

Her mom suggested that she attend a bereavement group for mothers who had lost a child. She thought that being with others who had experienced a similar loss would help because they would understand such a uniquely tragic pain. She had found one that was held every other Thursday evening at the large church near their subdivision, not far from where Larkin had gone to high school. When she was growing up, Larkin had been there several times when friends had invited her to summer camps and special events.

There was a meeting that night, and Larkin decided to go. She debated if it was too soon, but she had been mourning Maeve's death since her first ultrasound. She drove the short distance to the church and parked by the fellowship hall. She watched as other women filed inside, waving and hugging each other. She wondered how long it had taken them to feel . . . better? Normal? Functional? She wasn't sure if that was even possible. Larkin didn't know what she wanted or needed right then, other than understanding and being understood.

She sat in her car until after everyone else had gone inside. At 7:01, she walked into the room, hoping to sit in the back and just listen. But when she entered, all heads turned her way, and the women collectively invited her to join them in the circle of chairs at the center of the room.

About fifteen women attended that evening. Some looked to be close to her age, but there were mothers of all ages. The facilitator, who introduced herself as Elizabeth, looked familiar. She had platinum hair and stark, contrasting eyeliner. Larkin recognized the chiaroscuro figure as Elizabeth Hawks, the lecturer who had come to her school ten years ago to talk—or rather, not talk—about sex and who had never answered her question.

She motioned for Larkin to sit in the empty chair next to her and welcomed her to the group.

Elizabeth asked the group to introduce themselves to Larkin as they already knew each other well. Each mother told her their name, their child's name, how old their child was when they had passed, and how long it had been since they had died. Some gave the cause of death as well.

One had lost a child to cancer at age eight, another had lost a three-month-old baby to SIDS, and another had lost a child with a rare chromosomal abnormality who had died of a respiratory illness at age fifteen. Elizabeth's son had died by suicide at sixteen. They all shared with Larkin that the loss would never leave her—it would be with her daily—but they also reassured her that she would draw strength from others and find comfort in sharing memories of her child. They were all confident their children were now at peace and without pain in Heaven.

Some of them came to every meeting, while others only attended once or twice a year. Some would come only for an especially difficult birthday or milestone. They all took turns crying and comforting one another.

They discussed the blogs they had written and the poetry they had published about their children. One mother had posted photos and stories about her daughter on social media every single day since her passing four years ago so she would not be forgotten. They also shared Bible passages that had given them strength when their grief was especially crippling.

As Larkin listened to their stories, she hoped Maeve was also in Heaven with the other children. She hoped her grandparents and her pets that had passed were there as well. Larkin had never been sure about what happens when people die, and she had been content with not knowing before Maeve. She now understood why there was such a strong belief in this perfect and beautiful place among the clouds. How could you not believe there was something better after this life if your child died? If there wasn't a Heaven for the innocent lives that had been lost, how could any parent move forward with living their own life? The alternative, that they simply died and nothing more, would be unbearable to her.

After each member had spoken, Elizabeth asked Larkin to share her experience. It was still so fresh that she was beginning to regret coming, but she didn't know how it would ever get easier. She took a deep breath and shared Maeve's story with this group of strangers who were so willing to listen.

After she was done, there were murmurs of sympathy and understanding. A woman next to her reached out to pat Larkin's hand. Several walked over to hug her.

Elizabeth then asked each member of the group to share their favorite memory of their child, and Larkin listened as the other moms talked about their child's first steps, their first day of school, their love of music or painting or favorite movie or food. It was again Larkin's turn, and she was asked to share her favorite memory of Maeve.

When she closed her eyes and thought of her, the first image that flashed into her mind was Spencer softly crying as their baby gasped for breath. Then she thought of the hours she'd spent holding her lifeless body. There were so many difficult memories; she had to dig deep to remember holding Maeve for that brief time when she was breathing and Larkin could feel her heart beating. She realized then that Maeve had never even opened her eyes.

Larkin opened her eyes and told the group that being able to hold Maeve was her favorite memory. The mothers encouraged her to always remember that whenever the grief felt overwhelming. That was the only positive memory she was able to share from the few hours she'd had with her daughter. She wished desperately that she had more. She told everyone her hope was that someday, she wouldn't feel so utterly consumed by her grief.

Elizabeth reached over to lay her hand on Larkin's knee and said, "God doesn't give us more than we can handle."

Larkin replied quietly, "Then God doesn't know me very well."

The room fell silent, and Elizabeth removed her hand.

Larkin's voice shook as she continued. "I would have rather had an abortion than endure the last six months, after I found out Maeve would die. It has been frightening, isolating, and so very painful. And in the end, she would have died either way."

"We are sorry to hear that, but you know that would have been a sin," Elizabeth told her.

"And a loving God would have forgiven me for that sin," Larkin replied as she looked at Elizabeth with sympathy and thought, *And I am sure a loving God has forgiven your son for taking his own life. Isn't that also considered a sin? The God I know forgives people who are in pain and in despair. That is my God.*

Elizabeth said, "This experience will make you resilient, Larkin. You'll get stronger. You'll be glad you didn't abort her. It will be well with your soul." Her voice had an air of certainty.

"I don't want to be resilient," Larkin said firmly. "I want to be a mother. Or, rather, I *wanted* to be a mother. I wanted this baby so much, but now I'm too scared to ever try again and to have to go through this again." She paused and looked at the other women in the circle.

"You all agree with her, don't you?" she said, gesturing toward Elizabeth. "You all agree that even though I wanted an abortion for my mental and physical well-being, denying me that choice was really the right thing to do, don't you?"

The women in the group stayed silent and avoided making eye contact. The only sound in the room was Larkin's breathing becoming louder and more rapid. They shifted in their chairs uncomfortably.

"We know it must have been difficult for you," Elizabeth said calmly. "Making the right choice is hard sometimes."

Larkin ignored her and addressed the group again. "Look at me," she pleaded. "Please look at me and tell me this is what your God wanted. I don't believe He did. I can't accept that. I can accept that my daughter had a birth defect. I can accept losing her. I can't accept what people like you decided was best for me and Maeve without knowing anything about us other than that I was pregnant and believing I needed to stay that way. That's all that mattered to you, right? Right?"

When no one replied, Larkin stood and walked toward the door. She turned to the group and said, "I truly am sorry for your losses. I hope you can understand mine someday."

When she got back to her car, her hands were shaking as she texted Aubrey.

Are you free tomorrow?
I can be for you, friend. Tell me when and where.

CHAPTER 18

A large study of [HPV] vaccinated females showed a nearly 90% reduction in cervical cancer.
—The National Cancer Institute

Larkin was sitting in the corner of a coffee shop texting Spencer when she heard her best friend's voice.

"Larkin!" Aubrey yelled across the cafe, running toward her friend's table. They hugged each other tightly.

"Thank you for getting me my favorite latte," Aubrey said, as she sat down. She picked up the drink Larkin had ordered and took a sip of the iced lavender and vanilla concoction.

"Of course," Larkin said. Then, taking note of her friend's outfit, she said, "Nice hat."

Aubrey patted the knitted pastel pink cap with cat ears.

"I haven't seen you wear that since we were kids, and our moms took us to the Women's March in . . . 2017? Is this the new look all the medical students are going for? Seems a little warm for this time of year, but very cute."

Aubrey laughed. "Ha! You know I like to draw attention to myself. This way, all the lecturers call on me, and I can impress them with my superior knowledge. But I don't want to talk about me, okay? How are you doing? How is Spencer? I wanted to give you your space and respect your privacy, but it was so hard not to be with you through all of this."

"I know. It's been awful. Thank you for everything. Knowing you were there if I needed you was enough. Now I'm just trying to get out of bed every day. If I manage to shower and eat a little, it's a win."

"Yes, baby steps."

"Yeah."

"Oh, God. That was a stupid thing to say. I am so sorry. I wasn't thinking."

"It's really okay. That's the least offensive thing I've heard in the last couple of days."

"Is there anything I can do to help?"

"Just answer the phone when I need to cry. That's all. And I may be calling a lot. I hope when you're an ob-gyn, you can help other women in a similar situation. Help them not have to go through what I did."

"That probably won't be an option unless I want to lose my license or go to jail," Aubrey said. She told Larkin what she had learned in her medical law and ethics class about the rapidly changing laws and abortion restrictions in many states. State legislation had been introduced making it a felony to even say the word "abortion" to a pregnant patient. The law was expected to pass, making this action falsely equivalent to yelling "fire" in a crowded theater.

The database Dr. Beyer had mentioned was also likely to come to fruition on both the state and national levels. Any pregnant woman would be tracked until she delivered. If a woman had a miscarriage, she and her physician would be questioned by a task force to determine the legitimacy of the miscarriage. Plan B would likely be illegal soon. All forms of contraception would probably be targeted next.

"A lot of ultraconservative representatives and senators won nationwide in the last election, not just Jack Montgomery,"

Aubrey explained. "And while they're in power, they're going to change as much as they can as quickly as they can."

"This can't be real. I can't go through another pregnancy right now."

"Unfortunately, it's real. We can vote and protest as much as we can, but we're losing. We've been losing for over a decade. My advice to you is to get an IUD like I had while we wait for sanity to be restored."

"You don't still have yours?"

"No, I had mine removed."

"Didn't you get another one then?"

"No . . . my doctor couldn't replace it."

"Why not? It's not illegal yet, right?"

"No. It's not." Aubrey paused. "But you can't put in an IUD if there's no uterus."

Larkin looked at her quizzically. "What are you talking about?"

"I had to have a hysterectomy, Larkin. I have cervical cancer. I had surgery a few months ago and my uterus was removed, and now I'm on chemo, which is the real reason for my new fashion accessories. Thank goodness for false eyelashes and microbladed eyebrows," she said as she playfully pulled at her hat's knitted cat ears.

Larkin stared at her friend in disbelief. "What? No! Oh, Aubrey. Why didn't you tell me?"

"You had more than you could handle. I didn't want to add to that."

Yes, my friend knows me, Larkin thought.

Aubrey hadn't had medical insurance in college. Her parents had felt she was young and healthy and didn't need it. Fortunately, during college, she never needed to go to the doctor. She bought a health insurance plan when she started medical school and made her first appointment with a health care provider since she'd had her IUD placed in high school.

Aubrey told Larkin that during her first year of medical school, she'd started having frequent vaginal bleeding, which she'd never had before. She also had pain during intercourse. During her pelvic exam, the gynecologist collected a cell sample from her cervix for a Pap smear. He called a few days later to let her know that she had cervical cancer, and it had been caused by one of the most aggressive strains of the human papillomavirus. The doctor said it had been decades since he'd seen a case of cervical cancer in a patient so young—not since the HPV vaccine had been introduced.

The cancer had already spread from Aubrey's cervix to her uterus, making it necessary to have a total hysterectomy. Her ovaries were spared.

"I have homeless eggs now. Just tiny ovarian nomads wandering around my abdomen once a month with no place to go until they die and get reabsorbed in my abdominal cavity. On the plus side, I'll never have a period again. So, yay?" She shrugged.

"I'm so sorry, Aubrey."

"The irony of it all is that my mom didn't want me to get the HPV vaccine because she was convinced it would make me sterile. Joke's on her, right?"

"I remember. That's awful. Have your parents been helpful to you through all this?"

"We aren't speaking. My mom got furious with me for starting chemotherapy. She wanted me to take a holistic approach, and my dad supports her. She said I was poisoning my body, and I agreed—chemo is a toxic treatment. But it's likely going to cure me. My oncologist is optimistic. So, I told them I was taking my doctor's advice, and I was trusting the peer-reviewed research I had read, and they think I'm being naive. They told me not to call them until I came to my senses."

"Jesus. Do they even understand that if you had gotten the HPV shot, this could have been avoided?"

"Sadly, they don't have that kind of insight. But my brother has been amazing. He's taken me to a lot of my appointments. Lance stayed with me after my surgery. He's turned out not to be a total ass after all."

"It's great that you have him. And I'm so, so happy your oncologist is optimistic."

"Thank you. I can beat this. It was hard coming to terms with saying *adios* to my uterus, but if I'm cured, it's great."

"Well, it's not always a wonderful experience being pregnant."

"Yes, I thought of you a lot through all this. I still want to be an ob-gyn even though I'll never carry a baby myself. And I've decided to specialize in reproductive endocrinology and infertility. I want to help women who are struggling to get pregnant. Thank goodness there are some conservative senators that had children through IVF, so they haven't put any restrictions on it yet. I guess when it affects them personally, the rules are different."

"What would you have done if you were Dr. Beyer? If you had a patient carrying a baby like Maeve?"

"Unfortunately, the same thing. There isn't anything I could have done, as much as I would have liked to help. I'll keep voting, writing legislators, and going to protests. I'll keep trying and hoping a better alternative comes along. In the meantime, how are you taking care of yourself?"

"Well, there's the Zoloft. I'm on the max dose. And Spencer and our families have been great. My coworkers have been wonderful. It's just going to take a lot of time. I'll keep myself distracted with work. I probably need to find a hobby. I just need to keep my mind busy."

She told Aubrey about attending the bereavement group the night before and said that faith-based therapy wasn't for her.

Zoloft kept her from sinking deeper into the dark depths of her mind, but she still worried she could be completely consumed by her sadness if she didn't do something else. She just didn't know what that would be besides finding a good therapist.

After she and Aubrey talked for a few more hours, they hugged each other tightly and said goodbye. Aubrey promised that if Larkin ever needed anything, she would do whatever she could.

"Be careful what you promise—you never know what I might need." Larkin smiled. "And tell Lance thank you for taking care of you."

CHAPTER 19

Larkin stayed at her parents' house for a few more days until she felt ready to go back home. She spent that time sleeping, crying with her parents, and eating the assortment of comfort foods her mom made. Her mother tried her best to fill the void in her daughter's belly and her heart with chicken and dumplings, loaded potato soup, and endless peach cobbler with vanilla ice cream. When Larkin left, her mom packed plastic containers of food to take home to Spencer.

When she arrived home after a three-hour drive, Larkin kicked off her shoes and set her suitcase by the front door. It was quiet in the house. The fresh-cut sympathy flowers that had filled the den were now gone, surely long since wilted and dry. Two peace lilies flanked the fireplace, and the small silver box containing all that was left of Maeve rested in the same spot on the mantel.

When Larkin heard her husband's voice in the backyard, she walked through the house and onto the screened-in porch. She saw him in the yard, bent over as he looked into an open box that sat in the grass.

"Okay," he said, speaking to the box. "Not too much longer and you guys—chicks!—will be out of this place and into your new home."

Behind Spencer was a wooden structure that was about a foot off the ground and had a sloped roof. There were two small windows in front, outlined in white. A red painted door with a latch closure was between them, and a ramp went up the side to an area with a rectangular opening.

Larkin called out to him. "Hi! You've been busy while I was gone!"

Spencer excitedly jogged over to her as she stepped out of the porch and into the yard, warm spring grass under her bare feet. He grabbed her around her waist and kissed her slowly and gently. Then he looked at her with an exuberant smile. "I *have* been busy! I want you to meet the girls." Spencer took Larkin by the hand and led her over to the cardboard box where four small, fluffy chicks rested on a bed of paper towels with seeds scattered about. "This is Layla, Roxanne, Brandy, and Angie." He pointed to each chick individually and with certainty.

"How can you tell who's who?"

"I really have no idea yet. That's for you to figure out." He laughed.

She recognized the names from 1970s songs they both loved, and it reminded her of the day she and Spencer had met and talked for hours at the library instead of studying. He remembered that she'd told him she wanted to raise chickens someday. She asked Spencer when he had planned this, and she learned that he and his dad had searched the internet for information on how to build a chicken coop while she was visiting her parents. They'd built most of it while she was gone. He still needed to put up the bale of chicken wire that was laid by the coop.

"So, what do you think?" Spencer asked, his arms spread wide.

Larkin scooped up one of the chicks and held it to her cheek. "I think I love Brandy the most. Or maybe this is Layla?" She held the chick in her hands and stared at its face intently as it peeped. "Or maybe you are Roxanne?" she mused. Then her tone grew serious. "I love all of this, Spencer. I need this. Thank you."

"Great! They'll need a lot of love, and we have plenty of that! And in return, we'll have even more fresh eggs than what you already bring home from work. These chicks are Silkies. They're supposed to be very docile. They don't lay as many eggs as other breeds, but I also chose them in part because of their cuteness factor."

Larkin sat on the grass next to the box. The chicks were more active now, scratching and pecking at the seeds. As she stroked their backs, their feathers were silky to the touch, just like their breed implied, and they didn't mind being handled. Larkin could tell them apart by their distinguishing features, so she was able to decide who was who. Brandy was the chick with the most golden-brown feathers, Angie was the one with the whitest feathers, Roxanne was the one with the hint of red on top of her head, and Layla was the one who was the most aloof. Larkin patted Layla and murmured, "I hope you can ease my mind of worry. That's what you're supposed to do, right?" as the chick gently pecked at the ring on her finger.

As she played with the chicks, Spencer started installing the chicken wire fencing for the chicken run. Later, he would also install hardier fencing to keep out the foxes and coyotes he'd seen hunting in the fallow farmland behind their property. As he worked, she told him about her time with her parents and Aubrey, and Aubrey's diagnosis. She didn't mention the bereavement group.

Spencer told her to invite Aubrey over this summer. He would be completing the first year of his master's program soon, and he would be free for a couple of months. He planned to spend that time doing freelance accounting work for small companies that needed help with processing expense reports.

"You don't need to work, Spencer. I'll be back at work Monday, and I had enough sick and bereavement time to cover the days I missed."

"Nope. I want to work," he replied as he continued to busy himself with the fencing and tried to distract himself from a recent conversation that began to resurface in his mind.

While Larkin was gone, Spencer had gotten a notification, via the hospital app on his phone, that the billing statement was ready. Technology had made billing quick, efficient, and ruthless. He looked at the itemized list for the hospital equipment, obstetrician, anesthesiologist, medications, neonatal care, private room, and so on and so on. The list seemed never-ending. When he scrolled down to the bottom, the estimated patient responsibility was $8,573. Insurance was expected to pay over $33,000.

He had called the hospital's billing office to see if there was any way to lower the bill. When he spoke with the customer service representative, he asked, with a lump in his throat, if there was any sort of discount since their baby had died.

"I'm very sorry for your loss, sir, but the hospital incurs the same costs even if your baby dies. Usually more. We can't offer you a discount for that."

They were able to offer him a payment plan, but they expected it to be paid in full within twelve months. His parents had already given them a generous cash wedding gift last year, and he didn't want to ask them for more. He planned to open a credit card to pay off part of it and work to pay the rest in cash. He was thankful Larkin hadn't downloaded the app. He would never speak to her about the financial reality of having a dead baby.

He'd also received a statement from the crematorium: $599 for cremation, $150 for the silver memorial box, $25 for engraving. In total, they owed $9,347. He planned to work until he had covered all the expenses. If Larkin asked, he would tell her their insurance plan was taking care of it and leave it at that.

He remembered the sham couple who'd come into Jack Montgomery's office asking for a life insurance policy for their pretend unborn baby. He realized how helpful that would have been now, but the definition of "life" was apparently one of convenience for those in power, and no one asked or cared for his input. And no one cared that his baby was now dead. It was just important to others that she was born, no matter what the mental or financial cost.

He was pounding a metal stake into the ground with such force that Roxanne hopped from Larkin's hand and ran for safety, huddling with the other chicks.

"Are you alright, Spence?" Larkin looked at him with concern.

"What? Oh, yeah. The dirt was just a little harder in this spot, that's all." He stopped hammering and wiped sweat from his forehead with the back of his arm. "So, they are about three weeks old now. I'll be making the girls larger brooding boxes in the next few weeks. When they're six weeks old, they should be fully feathered and ready to move to the coop."

"And when will they start laying eggs?"

"About eighteen weeks, when they hit chicken puberty and become hens. Ha! Right now, they're pullets, young chicks that can't lay eggs. They won't lay as often as other breeds, but we should get at least a dozen or more a week. I'll put a few golf balls in their nesting boxes to get them used to the idea."

"Really? Golf balls? Was that your idea?"

"Nope. I've been reading about raising hens and getting tips. It's so interesting. I was also reading about how they'll lay fewer eggs in the winter."

"Because of the colder temperatures?"

"Because of less sunlight. The more sunlight there is, the more they lay."

Larkin started searching on her phone to read more about the egg-laying process: *Chickens are the most fertile when they have sixteen hours of sunlight a day. When ultraviolet rays from the red spectrum pass through their eyes, it stimulates the pineal gland and triggers hormones to be released into the bloodstream, stimulating egg production.*

"So, it looks like we could use artificial light to have them lay eggs when it gets darker, but I'd rather they just lay naturally. I want to give them a good life."

"Agreed," Spencer replied.

"I just want the chickens to be happy."

"That's what I want for you, Larkin."

PART II

CHAPTER 20

The estimated national maternal mortality rate in the United States is 23.8 per 100,000 live births—but it is about 55.3 per 100,000 live births for Black women.
—Centers for Disease Control and Prevention

November 1, 1988

"James, James . . . James! Wake up. I can't breathe." Gabby shook her husband's shoulder frantically. It was two in the morning, and the new father was groggy after being awoken from a deep sleep, something that had been elusive since bringing their son home from the hospital three weeks earlier.

"What's wrong?" James Davis Sr. said. "Is it the baby?" He stood in a panic and checked the bassinet where their newborn was sleeping peacefully, having just nursed an hour before.

"No, no, no. It's me," Gabby said. "I can't catch my breath. I don't know what it is. I need to go to the hospital. Please take me now."

He quickly put on his pants and shoes, gathered up James Jr., and stuffed a bag with diapers and wipes. His wife hadn't complained during her entire pregnancy despite vomiting almost every day and waking up almost every night with cramps in her feet. She'd been in so much pain that she'd quietly walked around the bedroom, trying to get some relief. She'd had a natural delivery and been fearless and stoic throughout. For her to be scared now—that scared him.

He took the baby and bag to the garage, strapped James Jr. into his car seat, and pulled the car up in front of their Memphis home. Then he ran back inside to help his wife of three years out the front door and down the brick stairs before helping her get into the car. She was still wearing her nightgown and had put on her robe and slippers. She was always immaculately dressed for her job as an English professor, but he knew her clothing choices mattered little to her now. She just wanted help.

The hospital was about ten minutes away. James desperately wanted to speed, but the fear of getting pulled over overruled his instinct. He didn't think a police officer would believe him when he explained why he was speeding—he figured an officer would only see a Black man breaking the law.

"How are you doing, Gabby?" he asked as he drove down the empty streets going just a few miles an hour over the speed limit, passing only an occasional service truck.

"Same," she said breathlessly. "Something just doesn't feel right. Please hurry." She tried to slowly inhale the cold night air coming in through the car's open window.

When they arrived at the emergency room, James pulled up to the double doors by the entrance and ran inside for help. A nurse brought a wheelchair to the car and assisted Gabby inside while James parked the car and got the baby.

When he walked into the emergency room holding his newborn son, who was still sleeping contentedly, the receptionist told him to go to bed fourteen. She buzzed him through the automatic doors leading from the waiting room to the seemingly endless exam bays, which were separated by curtains. As he made his way down the hallway, nurses and doctors hurried past him saying things like "GSW in Trauma one's pressure is dropping" and "MVA in two is stable and ready for Neurosurgery to take him upstairs" and "Going to need a chest tube in one!"

When he arrived at Gabby's bed, he heard a voice at the nurse's station say, "New arrival in bay six is here for shortness of breath. Pulse ox ninety-five on one liter, tachycardic at one-thirty. She's three weeks postpartum."

James pulled back the curtain, revealing the area where Gabby was lying. She had plastic tubing in her nose and was sitting up in the exam bed, resting. When James came in, her eyes fluttered open.

"Sorry to worry you, baby," she said softly.

"It's fine, but please don't do it again," he said as he kissed her hand.

"How is Junior?"

James held the baby close to her so she could rub his cheeks. "Nonplussed like his mother," he said.

"Mmm-hmm. 'Nonplussed.' Do you mean it as in the traditional definition of being 'surprised and confused and unsure how to react'?" she said between short, quick breaths. "Or the informal, modern North American definition being 'unperturbed'?"

"Whatever you think, professor. I am just a humble mathematics teacher."

James was happy he'd been able to briefly distract her. He rocked the baby in his arms and paced, wondering when she would be seen by the doctor.

The physician walked in a few minutes later and said to Gabby, "So, I hear you're having some trouble breathing?"

He didn't introduce himself or acknowledge James. James didn't care as long as he took good care of his wife.

"Yes, sir. It came on suddenly this morning."

"And you're a new mom, I see. First time? How is that going?"

"Yes. He's an easy baby. No problems."

"That's good. Any allergies? Prescription drug use? Smoker? Illicit drug use? Any history of anxiety or depression?" he asked as he listened to her heart and lungs.

"No. Nothing, although I have felt more anxious tonight," Gabby replied.

"Okay. Your lungs are clear. We'll check a few things, and I'll come back to talk to you later," he said as he twisted a knob on a green cylinder beside her. "Let's see how you do without this."

He stepped out and called to the nurse. "Let's get a chest X-ray, CBC, CMP, and urine drug screen in six."

James became mildly irritated. "'Six.' How about 'the patient in six'? Or 'Dr. Gabrielle Davis in six'?"

"James. I don't mind. I'm sure they're busy. I'm a PhD. Not an MD. I only ask to be called 'doctor' in the classroom. Let them do their job, baby."

A laboratory tech came in to draw blood for Gabby's labs. The nurse also helped her get to the bathroom for a urine sample, then put her in a wheelchair, and another tech took her to the radiology department for her chest X-ray.

James asked the nurse, "Why do you need a urine drug screen? Do drugs usually cause trouble breathing?"

"Just standard screening," the nurse replied.

While James waited for Gabby to come back, he talked to his little boy, who was starting to wake and root for his mother's breast.

"Hey, little man. She'll be back soon, okay? You know how much she wanted you? So much it hurt, and now that you're here, we love you so much it hurts even more. You're going to do great things with her mind and my good looks." He laughed as James Jr. started to fuss. "Yeah, I know . . . you got your good looks from her, too."

Gabby came back, and the nurse helped her back onto the gurney. "Ooooh. That made me dizzy," Gabby said, steadying herself using the bed railing.

"Make sure you're drinking plenty of fluids while you're breastfeeding. You're probably getting a little dehydrated," the nurse advised.

James helped place the baby on Gabby's chest so she could nurse as they waited for the doctor to return. He easily latched to his mother and immediately started to suckle. Outside the room, there continued to be a lot of chaotic conversations in the bustling emergency department.

Several hours later, the doctor came back to the room. He said, "Your labs look good, your chest X-ray was normal. Your heart rate is still a little fast, but new moms tend to be anxious."

"What about her oxygen level?" James asked.

"It's staying above 90 percent most of the time without supplemental oxygen. You don't have to make a hundred to pass the test. I'd recommend you call your doctor in the morning. Look into some treatment for postpartum depression."

"Even though I've never been depressed or anxious before?" Gabby pressed.

"Well, you said you have been now. It can happen with a new baby. Your symptoms acutely worsening this evening are likely from a panic attack."

"Okay. Maybe. I still just don't feel right," Gabby said.

"Life changes a lot after a baby. If you get worse, you can always come back. We never close. The nurse will be back with your discharge instructions."

The nurse returned a short time later with the paperwork. The discharge instructions listed the anxiety diagnosis at the top, followed by instructions to call her obstetrician in the morning. Neither Gabby nor James felt certain of the diagnosis, but according to the paperwork, Gabby was being sent home in good condition.

She still felt short of breath in the car. "Maybe I *am* anxious? Maybe I've been suppressing my feelings? I hope that's all it is."

When they got back to the house, James showered and got ready for work. He made some extra coffee for the commute to the high school where he taught. He kissed his baby boy on his head and his wife on her cheek as Gabby nursed James Jr. in bed. He said, "You're going to call the obstetrician first thing, right? And you are going to tell them you need to be seen today, right?"

"Yes, James. I will. Thank you for worrying about me."

"That's what love does to me. Makes me worry and makes me crazy, so now I'm crazy with worry. I'll only work a half day. I'll get someone to cover the afternoon. Can your mom come over this morning?"

"I'm sure she can. I'll call her. You go on to work," Gabby said. She coughed and held her chest. "Maybe I'm coming down with the flu or something."

"Call the doctor. Please."

"Yes, baby. As soon as they open. I promise. Love you."

"Love you."

Gabby's mom arrived later that morning and used her key to open the front door. She immediately heard James Jr. screaming from the back bedroom.

"Gabby! Honey!" she called out. "Are you in the shower? That's a hungry baby cry I'm hearing!"

She made her way toward Junior's persistent wailing. When she walked into the bedroom, she found Gabby's lifeless body face down next to the bassinet.

CHAPTER 21

"Cardiopulmonary arrest following acute pulmonary embolism" was the conclusion from the coroner's report.

Gabby hadn't died from anxiety. She hadn't suffered a panic attack. She'd died because blood clots had traveled through her bloodstream to her lungs. She'd had a rapid heart rate, her oxygen level had been borderline, she'd had shortness of breath, and she'd been misdiagnosed. Being Black and having recently had a baby, she was at a higher risk of postpartum complications—but she was misdiagnosed. She'd gone to the emergency room immediately, but she was misdiagnosed.

James Davis Jr. grew up knowing his mother had died from an embolism when he was a newborn. When he turned eighteen, his father shared the autopsy report with him, and he learned his father had hired a malpractice attorney, who agreed that the medical staff had missed his mother's diagnosis. A few years later, his father had received a large settlement from the hospital for their mistake.

James Davis Jr. knew his dad had wanted to take the doctor, the nurses, and the hospital's CEO to court—everyone he felt was to blame. His dad had wanted a jury and everyone else to know what had happened to his wife, but his lawyer convinced him to take the settlement and ensure his son's financial future. When he agreed, he reluctantly signed a nondisclosure agreement shielding the doctor and emergency room's errors from the public eye.

His father didn't spend a cent of the money he'd received in the settlement. He didn't want any of it. He raised his son on his teacher's salary, and they lived a comfortable life with the help of a modest payout from Gabby's life insurance policy. He saved the money for his son, both to fund his education and to help him do great things.

As James Davis Jr. unpacked his clothes when he moved into his dormitory at the University of Memphis his freshman year, his dad told him he wanted him to use his education to find a way to prevent others from dying like his mother had.

"I want you to be a different kind of doctor than the one who treated your mother," his dad said. "I want you to be the kind of doctor who listens to your patients. Who gets to know them as a human." He placed a stack of T-shirts in his son's dresser. "That doctor didn't know anything about your mom. He didn't know she was the first in her family to go to college. He didn't know she loved Shakespeare or that her doctoral thesis was on the modern iambic pentameter." He closed the drawer and turned to remove more clothes from a cardboard box sitting on the bed. "That doctor didn't know how much she wanted you and what a wonderful mother she would have been. She was just a number, not even a name." He shook his head at the recollection.

"I understand, Pops. I'll do my best and work my hardest. I want to make you proud," James reassured his father as he folded more T-shirts.

"Or you could be a lawyer," his dad continued as he hung his son's jeans on wire hangers. "Not a malpractice lawyer. I don't want you making money from others' mistakes." He turned and wagged a finger at his son. "Stop the mistakes before they happen. You need to be the kind of lawyer who fights to stop doctors from working twenty-four hours straight with no sleep, like your mom's doctor had done."

"Whatever path I take, I'll make you proud," James iterated.

His dad stopped working, cleared a spot on the bed, and sat down. "Sit here, Son," James's dad said as he patted the space next to him. "Please use your money and your mind to help other women like your mother. If you think you'll be silenced for raising your voice, then be thoughtful and quiet," James Davis Sr. implored.

"You want me to be quiet, Pops? Would Mom have wanted that?" James Davis Jr. asked with surprise.

"You can be quiet and still make noise—just make good trouble for those who need you. Their voices will raise up around you, and their volume, in both sound and number, will be rapturous." James's father put his hands on his son's shoulders and squeezed them gently. "Your mother will hear them. I promise you that."

James Davis Jr. wanted to honor his mother's legacy by helping other women, but he didn't think that being a doctor or lawyer would make a big enough impact. He didn't want to change things for *some* women. He wanted to change things for *all* women.

He changed majors several times during college, not because he failed any classes but because he dove deep into and relished every subject from history to chemistry to philosophy. He struggled with narrowing down what he wanted to do. He studied voraciously for all his classes and read about maternal morbidity and mortality during what little free time he had.

When he was younger, his understanding of pregnancy complications had been limited to the morning sickness and unusual cravings he saw on television sitcoms or overheard as his pregnant aunties commiserated. But in college, he read about pulmonary embolisms—both during pregnancy and after pregnancy—like the one that had taken his mother's life. The list of potential complications went on and on. There was also preeclampsia (which could lead to seizures), gestational diabetes, amniotic fluid embolism, and placental abruption. He also learned that these complications affected Black women at a higher rate than they affected others. The reasons were complicated and multifactorial, including implicit bias, structural racism, and lack of access to health care. He knew that fixing any of those issues on his own was beyond his reach. He had to think of another way.

During his classes, he preferred to sit in the last row of the lecture halls, sitting back in his chair, his hands folded in his lap, eyes closed as he listened. His professors became used to his aural learning style. He was never scolded for attempting to stealthily nap like some of his classmates would do. He would often abruptly open his eyes and raise his hand to ask a question before returning to his regular posture.

During his junior year, he listened intently in his anthropology class, eyes closed, as his professor discussed the differences in women's birth experiences compared to other mammals.

"There are major differences regarding how women experience giving birth compared to other mammals," the professor explained. "They labor much longer than other mammals and typically need assistance from an obstetrician or midwife to give birth, almost without exception, while other mammals labor and deliver alone."

The professor then advanced the slide to one titled "The Obstetrical Dilemma."

"In humans, infants' heads are large compared to narrow maternal hips," the professor continued. "This makes delivery challenging and can lead to mothers needing C-sections. According to the hypothesis, women need a wide pelvis to bear big-brained babies—those coveted 'good birthing hips' you may have heard of—but they also need a narrow pelvis to walk or run efficiently. It's an evolutionary trade-off."

James opened his eyes and raised his hand.

"Yes. What is your question?" the professor asked.

"Is this why human babies are born altricial?" James queried as the other students turned toward him, appearing confused by the term.

"Ah, yes. You've been studying," the professor replied. "That is what has been postulated. Human babies are born altricial—or helpless—compared to some other mammals because they cannot continue to mature physically and neurologically inside their mother as long as other mammals, due to the human mother's small pelvis."

"And this would be an example of antagonistic evolution, correct?" James asked.

"Correct. The need for bipedal locomotion necessitates a smaller pelvis, which can lead to a more challenging and risky childbirth process. Excellent questions."

James was astounded by the challenges and potential complications that prevented many women from having uneventful pregnancies and healthy babies. He saw these complications as failures of evolution, and he saw the solution as altering women's evolutionary course—not through natural selection but through deliberate genetic intervention.

He started focusing on his genetics and biology classes in college. He learned about the commonality of DNA between species and the various genetic pathways that determine our physical characteristics. He was fascinated by comparative biology, and his interests led him to pursue a doctorate degree. His area of focus was the development of reproductive organs in mammals and other animal groups and how they diverge over time.

In James Jr.'s view, avian species' reproductive mechanisms were far superior to humans' mechanisms. Chickens can make an egg within twenty-four hours, lay an egg in thirty minutes, and incubate the egg for three weeks before it hatches. A simple, beautiful, and easy process and so evolutionarily efficient.

He wondered if it was possible to tweak human reproductive evolution to make it better. *What if women could lay eggs like a chicken does?* he pondered one evening as he studied in the library. *Of course, the timeline would be much longer than that of a chicken. It would still take nine months or so for a baby to incubate and grow in an egg.* He laughed at the absurdity when he envisioned it as a reality.

But as he revisited the thought, he considered what it would mean for women. No more morning sickness, no swollen feet, no weight gain, no back pain, no fatigue. But more importantly, no risk of preeclampsia, no placental abruption, and no blood clots. So many benefits. So many complications could be avoided.

"Am I crazy or am I a goddamned genius?" he said out loud and smacked the table with the palm of his hand to the shushes of the other students. "What do you think, Mom?" He continued in a lower voice as he looked up at the heavens. "How would you have liked to have hatched me like a baby bird? Ha! I bet you would have loved that, and you'd still be with us. Dad would approve, I'm sure of that."

After finishing his doctoral degree several years later, he pursued traditional bench research and applied for a federal grant to establish his own lab in Knoxville, where he would study mandibular osteogenesis and facial morphogenesis using an avian model to better understand the sequence of events that led to the development of facial structures. He hoped to identify at a cellular level the cause of birth defects such as the cleft lip and palate that had affected two of his cousins. He hired Susan to be his first employee in 2016.

Dr. Davis knew he'd never get a government grant from the National Science Foundation or the National Institutes of Health for the kind of research he really wanted to do. He would have to use his trust fund money to pursue it on his own after hours. He spent every evening he could working in the lab alone, devoting his time to his foolish—or genius?—idea.

Other researchers had already done much of the groundwork for his project. The Human Genome Project, completed over a decade prior, helped James determine which segments of human DNA were responsible for developing female reproductive organs. Shortly thereafter, researchers used that same technology to analyze the entire genomic sequence of the red jungle fowl, an ancestor of domestic chickens. This gave James the information he needed to compare the two.

He knew the order of adenine, guanine, thymine, and cytosine needed to form the human uterus, fallopian tubes, and ovaries. He also knew the order needed to form the uterus (or shell gland), oviduct, and ovary in hens. Finally, he knew where that order was located within the species' respective genomes. He just needed to take the information from chickens and substitute it into the human code.

James had colleagues around the country who provided him with the supplies he needed and gave advice when he asked. He was vague about the purpose of his experiments, but he was revered in his field, and his colleagues respected the privacy of his research. Many knew bits and pieces of what he was doing, but he never discussed his ultimate goal.

For the next stage of his research, he ordered HeLa cells from a laboratory catalog. Containing the entire human genome, these cells are a staple of most scientific human cellular research.

James had gotten in the habit of talking to himself in the lab when no one else was there to keep him company. "Thank you for your contribution, Mrs. Henrietta Lacks," he said, acknowledging the Black woman whose cells had become integral to medical research. He gave a quick kiss to the package containing the cell line. "I hope my work meets your approval."

As he prepared the cell lines for storage, he said, "You know what, Mrs. Henrietta? They wanted to ban that book that was written about you. Yes, ma'am, ban it right here in Knox County. Some woman didn't want kids in high school reading about it. She didn't know the difference between 'gynecology and pornography,' as the author said." He shook his head in disbelief. "If someone ever writes a book about what I'm doing, I guarantee it will be banned and burned." He chuckled.

As James privately conducted his personal research, his public work with Susan thrived. They published multiple journal articles over the years, and he presented his work at national and international scientific conferences. He easily secured grants to grow his lab. Graduate students began requesting to collaborate with him, and he was happy to mentor them, though it slowed down his other commitments.

After working with Dr. Davis for sixteen years, Susan begged him to hire a research assistant. They had more than enough money from his grants, and the workload was becoming too much for her to continue alone. The visiting graduate students had all done well, and most left with a peer-reviewed publication under their belts, but they usually only stayed one or two years.

Dr. Davis advertised the position online and in journals that generated a lot of interest, but he was most impressed by a student who studied at the university where he worked and who would be graduating soon. Multiple professors had called him to praise her brilliant mind, her inquisitiveness, and her work ethic. Susan contacted the student and set up an interview with Dr. Davis.

Susan brought Larkin into the department conference room where Dr. Davis waited at the end of a large oak table surrounded by ten or so high-backed leather chairs. A whiteboard hung behind him. It was covered in research goals and deadlines.

"Very nice to meet you, Larkin!" He stood and extended his hand to her.

"You as well, Dr. Davis. I have heard so much about your work," Larkin replied. She took a seat in a chair across from him and clasped her hands in front of her on the table.

"So, tell me, why do you want to work here? Why are you interested in chicken beaks?" He smiled warmly as he leaned back in his chair, hands behind his head.

Larkin laughed. "Who knew chicken beaks could be so interesting, right?" She explained that her mother had a severe underbite when she was younger and underwent mandibular surgery as a teenager. Her jaw had been wired shut for six weeks as she healed, so she drank all of her food as thin purees through a straw during that time. Larkin had inherited the same mandibular prognathism, but fortunately, hers had been mild enough to correct with braces. Still, she'd wondered why and how it had happened. She'd started reading about other species and discovered that they developed similar defects. That spurred her interest in facial development across species, which led to an interest in the development of arms versus wings, nails versus claws, feet versus hooves, and the similarities of the genetic code and how the expression of different genes makes us who we are. She had fallen down a rabbit hole of evolutionary curiosity.

"Do you think we, as humans, are genetically superior to other species?" Dr. Davis asked.

Larkin said, "There is no doubt the evolution of our intelligence has led us to superior advances with literature, technology, theater, medicine, transportation, culinary arts, and on and on. And I don't know any cats who have created a cinematic masterpiece or dogs that have developed any lifesaving vaccines . . . but . . . may I say something completely nonscientific?"

"Yes, of course!" Dr. Davis encouraged her.

"If I get reincarnated, I'd love to be a duck."

"Why a duck?" He regarded her with genuine interest.

"I would be able to fly, swim, and live on land. The entire world would be accessible to me by my own power. And I have no sense of direction, but ducks have this amazing built-in navigation system. It's incredible. In that way, they are genetically superior to us."

"*And* you could lay eggs," Dr. Davis added.

"Very true! That would be amazing!" Larkin mused. She hesitated and then asked, "Have you ever thought about being reincarnated, Dr. Davis?"

"Actually, yes." He paused for a moment.

Larkin hoped he would elaborate, but she didn't want to be intrusive. She knew they had gotten off topic. She thought he would probably want to be a lion or a famous novelist or a leader of a country.

"I'd like to be reincarnated as a Black man in America," he said.

Larkin looked at him with raised eyebrows. She thought he might be joking, but she was quickly embarrassed by that thought.

Dr. Davis recognized the look of surprise on her face and explained. "I hope I was a Black man who tried with all my might to facilitate positive change in prior incarnations, and I hope to continue that until I succeed. I don't think my soul can rest until then."

And you just told him you want to be a duck. Way to go, Larkin thought. She was mortified.

"But a duck is a close second," he said with sincerity as he extended his hand to Larkin. "I'm looking forward to having you work with us."

CHAPTER 22

Platypus

Echidna

After almost a decade of working in the lab, Larkin was comfortable planning and designing experiments and working independently, although she continued working under the mentorship of her adviser, Dr. Davis. She'd planned on being alone all week as Susan was on vacation and the lab was between visiting graduate students. She was surprised when she arrived at work on Monday to find that all the lights were on and the door was unlocked.

"Good morning, Larkin!" Dr. Davis bellowed in his deep, joyful voice when she opened the door. "I beat you here!" he exclaimed as he was closing the door to the laboratory refrigerator.

"Good morning, Dr. Davis. This is a nice surprise. Did you come here very early?"

"No, I started working last night and I never left. Got too busy!" he said and sat down by the microscope table.

"Is this the private research Susan has mentioned to me? The project you've been working on for some time?"

"Yes, yes, yes! It's been coming along nicely. Since we don't have any students right now, I thought this would be a good opportunity to dedicate to my side hustle, as they say."

Larkin desperately wanted to know what his other research involved, but she stopped herself from asking. She sat down and busied herself with organizing and cleaning her lab station nearby.

"So . . . would you like to know what I've been working on all these years?" he asked as he rolled his stool closer to her.

Larkin's mouth was agape as she sat up straight to compose herself and then spun around in her lab chair. All she could do was nod in agreement. She was excited that he trusted her with this information.

Dr. Davis summarized his work over the past quarter of a century. He told Larkin how he'd perfected the method of splicing the segment of human DNA that codes for our internal reproductive organs and replacing it with a similar segment from a chicken. After many years of trial and error, changing substrates, and making sure he was splicing the DNA at the precise site, he had finally completed the exchange of genetic material. He'd repeated the process over and over to make sure it was reproducible—not a fluke. He had since been successful with growing the cells in culture and keeping the altered HeLa cell lines viable.

"So, you know, of course, that human females are XX and males are XY. And in humans, males have a gene on the Y chromosome, called SRY. It encodes a protein that causes a fetus to develop male gonads and prevents it from developing female reproductive structures." He paused to let her recall that information. "But did you know that in avian species, the females also have two different chromosomes, ZW, and the males are ZZ? Female avian species have genes that act like the SRY gene in humans, but their genes turn off the development of avian male reproductive structures."

"I didn't know that," Larkin replied. She was curious about what he hoped to achieve with this research.

He leaned forward, picked up a pen, and drew a cell with a few chromosomes dividing. "I wanted to develop a similar protein like humans and chickens have, but on the newly altered X chromosome that won't cross over between prophase I and metaphase I with an unaltered X chromosome and would essentially turn off that gene." He scribbled out one portion of a chromosome.

"So, your genetically engineered segment of the X chromosome would always be dominant in XX females? And that would be the genetic material that is always expressed?"

"Exactly!" He pointed the pen toward Larkin with emphasis, then twirled it between his fingers as he continued to explain. "The dominant human female gene would then continue to be passed down in females. And males who inherit the altered X chromosome from their mother would always pass this gene down to their daughters. And I did it, Larkin. I developed that protein. I've attached it to a fluorescent marker so you can see it. Look!"

He set down the pen and rolled back over to the microscope. He stood and gestured for her to sit in front of the fluorescent microscope, then turned off the lights.

"Do you see the area lit up in red?"

"Yes," Larkin replied.

"That's it! That's the gene for avian internal reproductive organs added to a human cell line." There was excitement in his voice.

Dr. Davis turned on the lights. "It's really amazing you were able to successfully do that, Dr. Davis, but I'm afraid I don't understand the practical application." Larkin looked up at her mentor.

"Ah, yes. One word, Larkin: platypus."

Larkin gazed at him with a puzzled look on her face.

"Well . . . two words, really. Platypus and echidna." He grinned like a child with two fistfuls of cash at a candy store.

"What do they have in common, Larkin?" he asked. He sat on the edge of the table, holding her by her shoulders.

"Mammals who can lay eggs?"

"That's right!" He gently shook her shoulders. "There are only two mammals that can lay eggs, but what if there were three, Larkin? *Three?*" he asked, holding up three fingers for emphasis.

Dr. Davis put his hands in his lap and continued explaining as Larkin slowly absorbed what he was telling her.

"If women could lay eggs instead of going through nine months of pregnancy, a lot of women would still be alive, my mother being one of them. That's why I wanted to do this, Larkin. That's why this was so important to me." He waited for a moment and took a deep breath before resuming. "I want women to have a better way to have babies—a way that gives them freedom, peace of mind, better health, better outcomes. They would have more control of their reproductive choices in a world where those choices are quickly being taken away. This won't help my generation or yours. It's too late for that. This would be for future generations. This is a long game of tweaking the evolutionary process."

Larkin thought about a future where Dr. Davis's world was a reality. Growing a tiny human inside of yourself—even a healthy one—is not for the faint of heart, as she knew well. She thought of all the strangers who'd approached her to relay their pregnancy woes when she was pregnant with Maeve. Stories of morning sickness, fatigue, heartburn, swollen feet, sciatica, high blood pressure, urinary incontinence, and so on and so on. And then there were the stories she'd heard about an ectopic pregnancy, a uterine rupture, or an emergency C-section for a shoulder dystocia. Larkin and Dr. Davis talked for hours about the possibilities and how it could work. Incubators could be adapted to house human eggs, just like incubators for chicks. Women would no longer spend nine months being incubators for their growing babies—they would be free to live and work without feeling bloated and exhausted. There wouldn't be multiple visits to the obstetrician anymore, and home deliveries would be commonplace.

They talked about how an embryo's growth would be monitored. Ultrasounds don't work with eggs because the shell's high calcium carbonate content doesn't allow ultrasound waves to pass. But an acoustic window could be created by cutting out a small portion of the shell, allowing ultrasound waves to pass so doctors could monitor the baby's growth and health. Once babies were full term, they wouldn't be able to hatch themselves because they would lack the egg tooth that chicks have, so they would be "hatched" by their parents or a midwife or a physician.

And they talked about how it would change abortion. If a woman wanted to terminate her pregnancy, there would be no need for an abortion—if a fertilized egg wasn't incubated, the embryo simply wouldn't grow. But unplanned pregnancies would rarely happen because egg production wouldn't occur without significant exposure to sunlight, just as Larkin had learned with her Silkie chickens. And if a mother decided to give the baby to a childless family for adoption, then the egg could be incubated for them and with them. It would change everything.

Larkin knew it would not have changed much for Maeve. She still wouldn't have survived her defect, but she would have had the chance to pass more peacefully. And the entire experience could have been less traumatic for both of them.

"What are the next steps of your research?" Larkin wanted to know.

"Well, now I would need a human test subject to see if my experiment is truly a success." Dr. Davis rested his chin in his hand. "I would have to alter a human egg and see if it would successfully fertilize. Then it would be implanted in the volunteer's uterus. Hopefully an embryo would grow, and that baby would have the altered genetic code. And if that baby is female, when the child grows to reproductive age, they should be able to lay eggs."

"And only the genetic code for internal reproductive organs would be changed in the embryo? Externally, everything would be the same?" Larkin asked.

"Exactly. The baby would look like any other female externally, but it should develop an avian reproductive system internally."

"And when the female is fully grown . . . how does she . . . mate?"

"Ah, yes. The old-fashioned way." Dr. Davis smiled. "The fundamentals of procreation would remain unchanged."

"Where do you plan to find a volunteer?"

"'Ay, there's the rub,' as Hamlet said. That will be a major obstacle," Dr. Davis acknowledged.

"I could do it," Larkin said, placing her hand on her heart.

"Larkin, I didn't confide in you hoping you would volunteer," he said. His tone was serious. "I would never ask you to do that after your experience with Maeve."

"I know, Dr. Davis, but how else would you find someone? You can't advertise for test subjects. And I want to help. I want to help *because* of Maeve. I want to be a part of this in a meaningful way. And I've been thinking about having another baby recently. It's been almost a decade. I think I'm ready."

"This is a decision not to be taken lightly, Larkin. If you're serious, talk to your husband. Give it some time. A lot of time. I have been working on this for over twenty-five years. We won't know if the experiment is a success for many more years." Then he quoted Shakespeare again. "'To climb steep hills requires slow pace at first.' I can wait."

"*Henry VIII?*" Larkin was not quite sure of her answer.

"Correct," Dr. Davis confirmed.

"'Our doubts are traitors and make us lose the good we oft might win by fearing to attempt,'" Larkin quoted.

"Impressive, Larkin, very impressive. My mother would love you for knowing that quote. But please, take your time and listen to those doubts. And a 'no' is expected and understandable."

That weekend, Larkin gathered eggs laid by the second generation of Silkie chickens to inhabit the backyard coop. Spencer had brought home Rhiannon, Cecelia, Lola, and Vera after the first chickens had passed away. They had all lived to be close to nine years old and had managed to survive a hawk attack and two fox attacks; Spencer had chased the predators away. The fencing he continued to modify and improve had also thwarted several black rat snakes from stealing eggs.

After placing the freshly harvested eggs on the kitchen counter, she joined Spencer, who was relaxing on their screened-in porch in the cool evening air. They held hands as they reclined in side-by-side lounge chairs listening to insects trilling and watching their hens scratch and peck at the birdseed and garden lime Spencer had laid down for them around the coop. He'd also put it in their water. The lime helped their eggs to develop hard, healthy shells. It also repelled pests and kept their water free of bacteria. Larkin watched an orange tabby cat in the distance, crouched and waiting to pounce on an unsuspecting field mouse.

"Spencer, I need to talk to you about something really important," Larkin said, squeezing his hand and turning her head toward him.

"Sure. What's up?"

"My IUD is due to be removed soon. We need to decide what to do after that. I can't get another IUD now unless we travel out of state. I've heard most gynecologists here will just turn a blind eye and won't report it if they know you got one somewhere else." She paused. "Or we can have your sister bring us condoms from Colorado like she offered, but I don't want her getting in trouble. I was scared enough when she snuck us a few THC gummies that time when she visited."

"Yeah. Probably not a great idea," Spencer acknowledged. "Or we could ask Aubrey if she can get you some birth control pills. She said she has lots of out-of-state connections. I think that's how she's been paying off her medical school loans the past few years." He laughed.

Larkin sighed and shook her head. Then she looked at her husband. "Should we just move, Spencer? Go to another state where birth control is still legal?"

"We could start over somewhere else, but if this becomes federal law, it won't matter where we move."

"Do you really think that will happen?" she asked with concern.

"I think there's a really good chance."

"We could just do something really stupid then."

"Like move to Canada? They don't want us anymore. They've been inundated with Americans. I'm sure they regret being so politely Canadian now." He laughed ruefully.

"No. Something really stupid."

Spencer looked at her quizzically.

"We could have another baby," Larkin said as she looked back toward the yard where the hens were still feeding.

"That's not stupid!" Spencer reassured her and sat up in his chair, turning his body toward Larkin. "That's great, but only if you're ready to try again."

"I'm ready. My therapist says I'm ready. She thinks I've made a lot of progress after seeing her for so long. I've been thinking about this for months, and it's time."

"But what if we get bad news again, Larkin? Do you think we can handle it?"

"I'm going to ask Aubrey to do my ultrasounds. If anything is wrong, she has other connections."

"I'll do whatever you want, Larkin. And I'm ready if you are. A baby would be wonderful."

"No matter what happens, we can handle this." She paused and then continued nervously. "I also had an interesting conversation with Dr. Davis this week that I've been thinking about."

Larkin detailed Dr. Davis's experiments and his motivation for pursuing his research, and she told Spencer she had volunteered to be his first test subject. Dumbfounded, Spencer looked at his wife.

"Why, Larkin? Why would you want to do this? It seems like something out of a sci-fi movie."

"It *is* science, but it's not fiction. This can work. But it's not a decision I am making just for us. Well, it is in the short-term, but in the long-term, it's for generations of women after us. This could be completely life-changing for so many women, including our future children."

Spencer held the sides of his head and rubbed his temples as if the information was too much to be contained within his mind.

"Okay, okay, okay . . . let me think about this. This is a lot to process."

"Thank you, Spencer. I need to talk to Aubrey as well. I'm going to need her help if we do this."

Aubrey was known to her patients and colleagues at the Knoxville Fertility Clinic as Dr. Abrams. She was hired after completing her fellowship and was excited about living closer to her best friend. She was still estranged from her parents, so she didn't feel compelled to live near them anymore. She had been declared cancer-free several years earlier, but her parents wouldn't know that unless Lance had told them. They never called her to ask.

Prior to having chemotherapy, she'd frozen some of her eggs in case she decided to have children one day. She hadn't yet met the right person to spend the rest of her life with, so they remained safely stored at a cryobank.

Not being able to carry a child herself made her more motivated to make it a reality for other couples who needed help. She knew she had chosen the right career path. Her office wall was covered with notes of profound gratitude and photos of parents holding their babies.

When her lifelong friend called to ask for her help with Dr. Davis's experiment, Aubrey immediately agreed.

"Aubrey, I don't think you've thought this through," Larkin said earnestly.

"You're right—I haven't. But you are asking me for a favor, and I want to help. That's all the thought I need to put into it."

"Aren't you putting yourself in jeopardy of losing your medical license? Ruining your whole career, which you've worked so hard for?"

"No one needs to know I helped you, Larkin. And I want to do it. Look, if I'd had access to an HPV vaccine, I wouldn't have had cervical cancer and I'd still have a uterus. If you would have had access to a safe abortion, you wouldn't have had to carry Maeve to term. Our lives have been changed forever by the decisions of others. It's your turn. It's *our* turn. I'm proud of you. And I think Dr. Davis's idea is amazing."

CHAPTER 23

January 22, 2041
The Tennessean
Hormonal birth control now banned in twenty-six states. US senators continue pushing for national ban led by Senator Jack Montgomery (R-Tenn).

It was close to midnight as Larkin lay on the procedure table at the fertility clinic with a paper drape over her legs, waiting for the Ativan to relax her prior to the egg retrieval. Spencer sat beside her, waiting for further instructions from Aubrey. The three of them had agreed to participate after weeks of discussion with Dr. Davis and Susan, but no one else knew what they had planned. The first experiments involving gene editing in human embryos had been performed in 2015, but they were strictly regulated after a lengthy moral and ethical regulatory process.

Dr. Parrish had removed Larkin's IUD two months earlier, cautioning that she couldn't offer any other type of birth control. Larkin reassured the doctor that she didn't want birth control right now. Once Larkin started having periods again, Aubrey gave her injections for two weeks to stimulate egg production and control the timing of her ovulation.

If the laws hadn't changed, Aubrey would have also been able to give Larkin oral contraceptives to help time the IVF process, but these were now considered a controlled substance and were only given under limited approval from a governing board after the physician submitted paperwork providing clear evidence that the contraceptives were being used to enhance fertility. Estrogen and progesterone were now as forbidden as OxyContin, fentanyl, and morphine.

Thirty-six hours prior, Aubrey had given Larkin a "trigger shot" of hCG, stimulating Larkin's eggs to mature. Aubrey hoped to get multiple eggs for Dr. Davis to use.

As Larkin focused on relaxing, Aubrey started an IV and placed her on a monitor. Susan had volunteered to help and would watch Larkin's vital signs during the thirty-minute procedure. Aubrey gave Larkin a short-acting sedative through the IV.

"How are you feeling, Larkin?" Aubrey asked as she squeezed her friend's arm.

"Pretty chill," Larkin mumbled sleepily.

"That's what we want," Aubrey said. "So, while you're in here, I'm going to send your hubby off to a room across the hall with this little cup and instructions to watch some quality porn of his choosing, which I am sure he has never done in his life." She looked at Spencer and winked. "He understands that this is for the greater good and is willing to make this sacrifice."

"Thanks, Aubrey," Spencer said awkwardly as he took the cup from her. Susan stared intently at the bare floor as Spencer walked past.

Aubrey and Susan then put on gowns, gloves, and masks. Aubrey sat at the foot of the exam table and inserted a long, thin tube with a suction device into Larkin's vagina. The tube was attached to an ultrasound probe so Aubrey and Susan could visualize the eggs.

"You might feel a little pinch," Aubrey said as the device punctured the vaginal wall and moved toward the ovary. Larkin didn't seem to notice, so the mild sedative had been successful.

Aubrey was able to suction twelve eggs from both ovaries. She placed them in test tubes and handed them to Susan.

"Nice job, Larkin. We're all done for now."

Spencer walked into the room as they were finishing up, holding the cup by its blue lid. Arm outstretched, he handed it to Aubrey without saying a word.

"Why, thank you! Come again!" Aubrey said cheerily, waving her hand as she took it from him. Spencer rolled his eyes and mumbled something under his breath. Susan failed to hold back a snort. She said she needed some water as she covered her mouth to unsuccessfully stifle a laugh. She handed the harvested eggs back to Aubrey and exited the room as fast as she could.

"Larkin will be a little drowsy for a bit. Please stay with her until she perks up, then help her get dressed. Make sure you tell her my hilarious joke when she wakes up," Aubrey instructed Spencer.

"Sure. Hilarious," he replied.

Aubrey took the eggs and the semen sample to a room at the end of the hall where Dr. Davis waited in the embryology lab with Susan, who had finally stopped laughing.

"Time to make a baby, Dr. Davis," Aubrey said as she handed him the test tubes containing the eggs.

"Excellent. Thank you," Dr. Davis said. He used a pipette to remove fluid from the tubes and placed it on a glass slide.

Dr. Davis examined the egg samples under the microscope and chose the ones of the appropriate maturity. He then injected them with modified genes that would bind to the gene segment he wanted to remove. The old gene would be spliced and replaced with the new genetic material. He was able to complete the process for nine of the twelve eggs.

While he prepared the eggs, Aubrey began processing the sperm sample. She used a special solution containing antibiotics and protein to "wash" the sperm and then placed it in a centrifuge in the corner of the lab to separate the healthy, motile sperm from the poor swimmers. She repeated the process several times to get the healthiest sperm for fertilization. The concentrated sample was then placed in a special medium to nourish it prior to being transferred to the egg.

Each egg was placed in a petri dish of culture medium along with a sample of sperm before being incubated.

"Don't you need to inject the eggs directly with the sperm?" Susan asked Aubrey, recalling what she'd learned in medical school.

"Intracytoplasmic injection is another option to fertilize the egg, but since Spencer and Larkin don't have fertility issues, we can use this more conventional method and expect the same success rate."

Once the process was complete, Dr. Davis placed the petri dishes, labeled "Dr. A. Abrams," in the lab incubator. Aubrey would check on them the following day.

After they had completed the process, Dr. Davis, Aubrey, and Susan walked back to the treatment room, where Larkin was now dressed and waiting with Spencer.

"So far, so good," Dr. Davis reassured them. "We'll monitor how they're growing every day, and on day five, I'll check to see if the gene transfer was a success."

"And then we'll place one of the eggs back into Larkin and hope for great news," Aubrey added.

"That's one small step for woman, one giant leap for womankind," Larkin said softly.

Aubrey checked on the embryos' development every day and was pleased that all the specimens were dividing well. On day five, she, Larkin, and Dr. Davis once again met in the fertility lab in the middle of the night. Dr. Davis removed a petri dish from the incubator and brought it to the IVF chamber, which looked like a clear plastic box with armholes on either side and a microscope in the middle. Humidified air inside the chamber kept the samples in the most ambient conditions. He placed the petri dish under the microscope and got the specimen into focus.

"Want to see how they're coming along, Larkin?" Dr. Davis asked.

Larkin eagerly nodded, and he got up from the stool so she could see. Under the microscope, she saw a round cluster of about one hundred cells.

"It made it to the blastocyst stage. It's perfect!" Larkin exclaimed.

They checked the other specimens, which had all divided and grown into blastocysts as well, some further along than the others. They would be ready for transfer tomorrow.

"You have a plethora of good specimens to choose from, Larkin. I'm going to take a small biopsy from one of the blastocysts to confirm that the transfer worked by fluorescing the desired segment. I'll also be able to tell if the chromosomes are XX or XY. Do you want to know, or do you want to be surprised about whether it's a girl or boy?" Dr. Davis asked.

"I want to know," she replied without hesitation.

Dr. Davis sat back down in front of the microscope and used a small laser to puncture the trophectoderm, the blastocyst's outer layer. He removed about eight cells, which would later form the placenta, and placed them in another petri dish. He then added the medium that would fluoresce the genes of interest.

He brought the specimen over to the fluorescent microscope he'd brought from his lab and placed it on the microscope stage.

"Can someone turn the lights off for me?" he asked.

Aubrey turned off the lights, and they waited while he examined the cells. Dr. Davis saw one of the chromosomes with a brightly lit section. He started laughing—a deep, exuberant laugh. "It worked. It worked!" he exclaimed, standing and clapping his hands. Then he looked up and, with clasped hands, said, "Mom. It worked. Thank you." Looking at Larkin and Aubrey, he added, "And it worked because of both of you. Thank you. Thank you!" He turned to Larkin. "If this is the embryo you want to transfer, then I can also tell you the sex, if you would like."

"Let me get Spencer on the phone so you can tell us together." She dialed Spencer and put him on speakerphone. "Hi, Spence!" she said. "Are you ready to be a dad again?"

"Yes!"

Larkin nodded to Dr. Davis.

"Congratulations to you both! You're going to have a baby girl."

Larkin suddenly froze at the memory of Dr. Beyer flatly telling her, "Females tend to have a higher rate of anencephaly compared to males. About three to four times as high." Her heart started racing, and she felt like she wanted to run. But run to where? She didn't know, other than to get away from the thoughts in her head. So, she simply sat, unmoving.

"That's fantastic news, Dr. Davis," Spencer said over the speaker.

"Hi, Spencer. It's Aubrey. Tomorrow will be the implantation, and then things will be much simpler after that."

"Are you okay, Larkin?" Aubrey asked since her friend had been so quiet.

"What? Oh, yes. Just processing it all. It's all very exciting."

"Alright then. Get some rest. I'll be all up in your nether regions again soon," Aubrey teased.

Larkin had been taking Viagra to thicken the lining of her uterus and improve the chances of implantation. Progesterone had traditionally been used for this purpose, but acquiring it covertly had become an impossibility. Viagra, however, was easy for Spencer to obtain from his doctor with as many refills as he wanted. Numerous studies had shown that it was a successful alternative for improving the chances of embryonic transplantation. Larkin took his prescription under Aubrey's instruction.

The other eight embryos were transferred to a cryopreservation unit Dr. Davis had bought for the lab, and they could be thawed for use later if needed. The ninth one would be implanted in Larkin the next day.

Larkin lay back on the fertility clinic's exam table with the paper drape over her legs and held Spencer's hand. Aubrey took a soft, flexible catheter containing the selected embryo and, with ultrasound guidance, located the desired spot in Larkin's uterus and placed the embryo. The whole process took only a few minutes.

"That's all there is to it," Aubrey said as she helped Larkin sit up. "Now we wait two weeks and check a pregnancy test. You may have a little cramping and spotting, but that's normal."

Larkin remembered the first and only time she had taken a pregnancy test—in the bathroom at work. She recalled that she'd been in shock at first, but that feeling had quickly changed into excitement and a deep desire to have the baby that, just a short time before, she hadn't even known existed. The feelings of pure want that washed over her in that moment had taken her by surprise, and she felt that wonderfully familiar way again.

Waiting two weeks was both exciting and excruciating for Spencer and Larkin. On the eleventh day, Larkin had some mild abdominal cramping and was bleeding lightly. She started to panic.

"Larkin, Aubrey told you this might happen, remember? I think she called it implantation bleeding. Text her if you're worried," he urged.

"I'm sure she'll say everything is fine. And it probably is, but I'd feel better if I took a pregnancy test now. I won't be able to think of anything else for the next few days if I don't."

Spencer agreed to drive her to the pharmacy. They looked in the family planning section for pregnancy tests. They were normally next to the feminine hygiene products, but they couldn't find anything on the shelves.

Larkin walked up to the pharmacy window and saw several shelves housed behind a locked plastic box filled with decongestants and pregnancy tests. She asked the young tech who was standing at the register if she could purchase a test. She thought teenagers must have been stealing them.

"I'm going to need a photo ID, and the pharmacist will take down your information. The restroom is to the left. You can do your business in there and then bring it back in this." The tech handed Larkin a small plastic biohazard bag. "We'll call you back when we get the results."

"What are you talking about? I want a pregnancy test, not the Sudafed. Why does the pharmacist need my ID? And why am I leaving the test here?" The request sounded absurd to Larkin.

"It's the state law that passed recently. Or maybe an executive order or something." The tech shrugged her shoulders.

"*Another* ridiculous law? And the pharmacist would call me? With my results? Why?"

"So we can make sure to have your result in the state database. If it's positive, the health department will contact you tomorrow to schedule an appointment with an obstetrician. And I'm required to inform you that failure to appear for your obstetric appointment could result in fines or arrest. May I have your ID?" The tech extended her hand, palm up, and waited for Larkin to hand over her license.

"What the fuck? No, you can't have my ID."

"Please don't curse at me. I don't make the rules, ma'am." The tech drew back her hand and tapped her fingers on the countertop.

"You may not make the rules, but she isn't giving you her ID. This isn't your business," Spencer said angrily.

"Once you request a pregnancy test, it now legally makes it my business."

"We don't want one anymore," Larkin stated, crossing her arms in front of her.

"Then I need to inform you that you both are on our security cameras, and we'll have to report this incident to the state." The tech pointed to the security camera that was positioned above her register.

Larkin looked at the camera, stretched her arm toward it, and extended her middle finger. Spencer grabbed her by the other arm, and they left the pharmacy with Larkin continuing her defiant gesture until they were out the automatic doors.

As they walked back to their car, she texted Aubrey and told her about the cramping, the spotting, and the pregnancy test. Aubrey came to their house a short time later and handed Larkin a pregnancy test from her office. Because every patient at the fertility clinic wanted to be pregnant, those tests weren't monitored yet.

Larkin hugged Aubrey and thanked her.

"You're welcome. Now go pee on your stick." Aubrey nudged her friend.

Larkin went to the bathroom and squatted over the toilet, holding the pregnancy test between her legs. As she focused on urinating, she thought about what a strange and unrefined way it was to learn about one of life's most exciting and life-changing events. She listened to her urine dribble into the ceramic bowl and splash onto the test strip. The ridiculousness of the process took her mind off her experience at the pharmacy.

She laid the test on the bathroom counter and stepped out to tell Spencer and Aubrey the results. She was overwhelmingly relieved to learn she was still pregnant, and all three joined together in a hug as Larkin cried softly.

A few days later, Larkin asked Aubrey to confirm with a blood test, and she was grateful when the results were also positive.

Several weeks later, after the fertility clinic was closed for the day, Aubrey did a transvaginal ultrasound on Larkin to make sure all was well. She was able to see the gestational sac, which was located in a good position in the uterus.

"So far, so good, Larkin. I want you and Spencer to come back here in about two months so we can do another ultrasound—not a transvaginal one. Just a standard ultrasound."

"And this is when you can tell if she's okay?"

"She's okay now, Larkin. But I'll be able to get a good idea of whether everything is anatomically normal."

"Two months seems like forever," Larkin murmured.

"Seven weeks will be the earliest we can check. She'll be at about twelve weeks gestation. Let's check then."

"Thank you, yes. I'd like to check the earliest we can."

"Will do," Aubrey said as she smiled at her friend reassuringly.

Exactly seven weeks after Larkin's initial ultrasound, Aubrey let Larkin and Spencer into the fertility clinic after hours. Larkin had convinced herself something would be wrong. She was afraid to be optimistic and prepared to be devastated again. She couldn't make herself feel excited or hopeful, and she felt it was better this way. She decided that if she was already deeply entrenched in a pit of disappointment, any bad news would be less painful since she couldn't fall much further into despair.

And, if something was wrong, Larkin would go anywhere she could if she needed an abortion. No one from the pharmacy had contacted her yet, so she didn't think they had been able to identify her from the camera footage, and Aubrey, of course, hadn't reported her pregnancy in the database. Larkin had heard that some clinics in states where abortion was allowed had started helping out-of-state patients, ignoring mandates from other legislatures that they were required to report those women. Their states' rights were still their own for now.

Larkin lay on the table with Spencer next to her as Aubrey squeezed the familiar cold, viscous substance onto her bare lower abdomen. She stared at the tubular lights flickering overhead and concentrated on their harsh buzzing noise rather than looking at the monitor. She heard the heartbeat right away, as she had for Maeve, and every muscle in her body tensed as she steeled herself for the bad news.

"Larkin, look. Look at your baby," Aubrey urged. "All is well."

Larkin raised her head and looked at the monitor as Aubrey pointed to the baby's arms and legs and heart and beautifully developing brain. She was perfect. She was whole. Larkin felt herself being lifted from the deep emotional hole she had been ensconced in for a decade.

"I don't believe it. In the best way, I don't believe it," Larkin said as she wept.

Spencer hugged her and covered her face in kisses, and then he hugged Aubrey.

"What's next?" Spencer asked Aubrey. "Besides getting a nursery ready and pampering Larkin and choosing a name?"

"Well, my work here is done. Now you'll make a new-patient appointment with Dr. Parrish, and you can be seen by a doctor during daylight hours instead of under the cover of darkness." Aubrey laughed.

Larkin's happiness was momentary. She was anxious throughout the pregnancy, convinced at every stage that something awful was going to happen. She was scared to buy anything for the nursery and declined any offers for a baby shower. She would not allow herself to enjoy being pregnant because she had convinced herself that something bad would happen to the baby if she let her guard down. Dr. Parrish couldn't provide enough reassuring words, perform enough ultrasounds, or do enough laboratory tests to stop Larkin from catastrophizing. She started taking Zoloft again to help with her anxiety and went to her therapist weekly. Spencer and Aubrey also tried to put her mind at rest, but it was constantly racing with memories of being pregnant with Maeve. She could not and would not allow herself to simply relax as she prepared for bad news. Her entire pregnancy and labor were just as fraught with fear as the last one.

It wasn't until January 2, 2042, at 9:15 p.m., when she, Spencer, their parents, and Aubrey welcomed a healthy seven-pound, seven-ounce Ava into the world that Larkin could breathe a sigh of relief.

PART III

CHAPTER 24

June 24, 2047
AP News
President Montgomery praises passage of a nationwide ban on abortion and birth control on twenty-fifth anniversary of Dobbs decision

Abortion rights activists working rapidly with international suppliers to traffic birth control and abortion pills into the United States

"Slow down, Jameson! I can't breathe!" Ava giggled. She and Jameson were running in the backyard. They chased after Cecelia, who tolerated their excited squeals better than her avian sisters did. They warily remained near the coop to quickly retreat inside if needed. When the children finally caught her, they sat on the ground, taking turns gently stroking her feathers and softly speaking to her like they'd speak to a baby sister they wanted to protect. They both loved the chickens and desperately wanted the chickens to love them back. Fortunately, Silkies are a very friendly breed. Once the kids sat down and were calm, the other chickens approached them.

Ava was now five years old. She was a bright and curious girl with large hazel eyes and light brown hair, like her mother.

She had also inherited her mother's persistent inquisitiveness. Spencer and Larkin had nicknamed her the Duchess of Whyvaria because of her relentless need to know immediate and precise answers to every question she posed. "Because" or "I don't know" were unacceptable in the Duchy of Ava.

Jameson was almost four. He and his mother, Aubrey, visited often, and he had adopted Ava's habit of asking *why?* He seemed to have imprinted on Ava, following her everywhere like a gosling follows a mother goose. He got up when she did, walked when she did, and ran when she did, always just a step or two behind. He was quieter than Ava, content to be in her presence listening to and learning from her. He never threw the kind of tantrums his mother had been warned he would at this age. When he was upset or scolded, he would simply hold his head down for a bit, quietly thinking, and would return to playing after a short period of reflection.

"How do chickens make the eggs?" Ava asked Larkin. She petted Lola while Jameson held Cecelia.

Larkin, who was cleaning the coop, replied, "Well, they start with the yellow part, the yolk, in a special part of their belly called the oviduct, and that's where the white part of the egg is made as well. Then the hen makes a hard shell around it. The whole egg makes a perfect package to feed and protect a growing baby chick. But our eggs don't grow baby chicks, so we are able to use them for food instead."

"Why don't they grow baby chicks?"

"Yeah! Why?" Jameson interjected.

"Because they don't have all the instructions they need to make a baby chick. The hens have half the information. The rooster has the other half, and we don't have a rooster."

"What kind of instructions?"

Larkin thought briefly and replied, "Remember when your dad and I were putting together your big-girl bed in your room?

We needed to follow instructions to show us how to put it all together."

"How does the rooster give the hen the rest of the instructions?"

"Well . . . chickens kiss, but in a very different way from how people kiss. They both have an area of their private parts called a cloaca, and when their cloaca 'kiss,' the rooster is able to give the hen the rest of the information needed to make a baby chick."

Ironically, cocks don't have cocks, Larkin mused. *And human embryos start with a developing cloaca, and if it doesn't disappear during development, they develop an anomaly called mermaid syndrome,* she recalled from her comparative biology course, one of the seminal educational moments that had cemented her belief in evolution.

She hoped she'd explained it well enough for Ava to understand. The sex and mating part really wasn't the hard part—it was relatively simple to explain with chickens—but the complicated embryology and genetics were too much to grasp at her age.

"Oh. Okay," Ava said as she thought about this new information. "How long does it take to make the egg?"

"Hens are fast! It usually only takes them a day to make an egg. That's why we can gather the eggs today and there will be more in two or three days. Silkies don't lay as often as other chickens. Some chickens can lay every day."

"Does it hurt them to lay eggs?"

"I've read that if the chickens are really young, or the eggs are really large, it can hurt."

"Aww. Poor Silkies!" Ava said as she petted Lola and kissed her head. Jameson copied her and kissed the top of Cecelia's fluffy head.

"But since they lay smaller eggs and they are older now, I don't think it hurts as much—if it hurts at all."

"And why are the eggs different colors?"

"That's all in the instructions, too! The color of their egg is partly caused by their bloom—that's the coating on the outside of the egg that keeps germs out. Did you know you can tell what color egg a chicken is going to lay by looking at their earlobes? The color of the earlobes is usually the color of the egg."

Jameson and Ava started looking for the earlobes on the hens they were holding. Larkin picked up Rhiannon and sat down with them.

"What color eggs does Rhiannon lay?" Larkin asked them.

"Brown!" they answered in unison.

"That's right. So, look here," Larkin said as she brushed the soft feathers away from the side of Rhiannon's head. "And what color is her earlobe?" She showed them.

"Brown!" they said again and laughed.

Ava and Jameson both found white earlobes on their hens. They were ecstatic over this new piece of information, along with the discovery that chickens with green eggs would have green earlobes. They then picked up Vera and were able to find her reddish-brown earlobes. Next, they asked to go to the neighbors' house to investigate their chickens' earlobes.

"I'm sure we can go over later," Larkin said. "Let's wait until we see them outside." She was amused that this was so fascinating to them, but she also knew she would have loved learning all of this when she was younger.

Aubrey sat on a bench under the shade of a live oak tree watching the children play and listening to their conversation and laughter. Larkin went inside and came back with iced tea for them and ice water for Ava and Jameson, who were unbothered by the heat of the already sweltering summer morning.

Ava and Jameson ran over to get their drinks with Jameson still cradling Cecelia in his arms. Larkin took both cups and handed one to him as they sat on the grass to drink. He was almost as big as Ava with curly blond hair, chestnut eyes, and golden brown skin.

"Thank you so much, Larkin," Aubrey said sincerely as she took a glass of tea from her.

"You're welcome! I hope it's not too sweet. My mom made it earlier in the week when she was watching Ava."

"Oh, the tea is great, but I was thanking you again for Jameson. I know I've thanked you a million times already, but it feels like it will never be enough."

"*Mi uterus es su uterus.*" Larkin laughed. "I was more than happy to help."

Larkin had suggested being a surrogate for Aubrey before Aubrey had even thought to ask. In hindsight, Larkin's pregnancy and delivery with Ava had been thankfully easy and uneventful, and she wanted that experience again. She especially wanted it for her friend. Aubrey hadn't been sure if she would ever use the eggs she had frozen before her chemotherapy treatments, but it was life-changing when Larkin made such a generous and selfless offer. Aubrey's frozen eggs had undergone the same genetic splicing procedure as Larkin's eggs, and Jameson carried the same gene as Ava on his X chromosome. If he had children someday, he would pass the gene to his daughters.

"You did an excellent job of being peppered with questions. You must be mentally exhausted," Aubrey said to Larkin as she sipped her tea.

"Exhausted but happy."

The three siblings who lived next door had joined Ava and Jameson in the backyard. The kids put down their cups and asked again if they could go to the neighbors' house to see their chickens. Their mothers agreed to let them go as long as they stayed in the backyard and came right back after completing the earlobe inspection. Aubrey and Larkin watched as their children excitedly ran the short distance.

"It's hard to believe, isn't it? That we have these two amazing humans to raise?" Larkin asked.

"It is," Aubrey said. "I never thought I would have children. It's been a good dream, and I never want to wake up."

"After Maeve, I felt like I was in a bad dream I couldn't escape. And now, I just look at Ava and I'm shocked that this is my life."

Ava and Jameson ran back to them, both yelling "Mama!" and "Mommy!" over and over. They stopped, out of breath, and told them, "All brown! Brown eggs! Brown earlobes!" Their voices were filled with pure, unadulterated enthusiasm.

Larkin praised them. "Great job, guys! Fantastic investigative work!"

"Can we play in my room now?" Ava asked.

"Sure!" Larkin replied.

Ava grabbed Jameson's hand as they ran inside the house. As the back door closed behind them, Aubrey asked Larkin, "Have you and Spencer decided when to tell her?"

"Yes. When she's closer to puberty. We still have some time."

CHAPTER 25

Summer 2047

James Davis Jr. entered the Beloved Ones Memory Care Facility in Memphis with books, chocolates, a new pair of pajamas, and warm nonslip socks. As he walked down the hallway, several residents waved or reached out to him, seemingly confident that they recognized a familiar face. An elderly woman wearing a turquoise kaftan buttoned up the front slowly made her way down the hall using a walker with tennis balls embedded in the back legs, nodding and smiling at James.

It made James wonder how it was determined which tennis balls would be worthy of Wimbledon's grass courts, which would be used to help the elderly with their mobility, which would keep chairs and desks from scuffing the floors at elementary schools, and which would be lobbed into a lake for golden retrievers. They all had their own evolutionary path. All served a worthy purpose, but with very different destinies.

When he arrived at his father's room, there were two balloons taped to the laminated biography hanging to the left of the door. In a few paragraphs, it summarized the highlights of his father's life. His parents' wedding photo was above it, the same framed photo he had in his office. One of the nurses had placed a thin plastic banner with a cheery "Happy Birthday" above the door.

James set the items he'd brought on the bed, which was covered with a blue plaid comforter. His dad dozed in a large recliner. He had a small pillow behind his head and was softly snoring. James grasped his knee and gently shook it. "Pops. Pops! I'm here."

His father woke up and instantly beamed with delight, the wrinkles in his face coming to life around his eyes and forehead. He held out his arms for an embrace.

"My son. My pride. My joy. I need nothing else today."

"Well, I hope you need your favorite chocolate, too, because I had to smuggle it past the nurses," James said as he took a seat on the bed.

"Ah, yes, I guess I did need a little something else today. Thank you, son."

"Happy ninetieth birthday. And many more," James said as he unwrapped a few dark chocolates with sea salt and gave them to his father.

"I'm ninety today?" he asked with surprise, then repeated softly to himself, "Today I'm ninety. Today I am ninety."

"Yes, Pops, that's right."

"And you are here because I am ninety?"

"Well, yes, but I also visit at least every two weeks."

"You're a good son."

"Thank you. I try."

"Is your mom here, too?"

"In spirit, yes. Always."

"Well, that's nice."

James did visit every two weeks or more, always bringing books and poetry to read to his father. He would also update him on his research. He wasn't sure how much of it his dad understood, but he listened intently to every word, and it helped James to talk about it out loud, to organize his thoughts and decide on the next steps.

He had previously told his father that harvesting eggs and altering them in vitro, as he'd done with Larkin, was a cumbersome and expensive process. He needed to develop a way to make the process affordable and accessible to all women, and it would be essential to simplify the procedure for it to work on a wide scale. It was becoming more pressing with the current laws in place.

Shortly after Larkin became pregnant with Ava, he began working on an intramuscular injection using a viral vector that would selectively bond to human eggs, inject the genome into the cell, and complete the splicing process in vivo. The technology had been available for decades and had been used to develop several successful vaccinations. Both Susan and Larkin were putting in additional hours to assist in his work, and he believed he had succeeded after several years of experimentation.

The timing was right—women were desperate for change. Women's rights groups were successfully smuggling oral contraceptives, Plan B, misoprostol, and mifepristone from Canada, Mexico, and Europe, but they usually only got into the hands of the wealthy and the privileged. If you were poor and pregnant, your options were limited, and rumors of back-alley abortions were becoming commonplace once again.

James Jr. asked his father how to get his scientific breakthrough into the hands of the general public and how to convince them it would work. First, he would need to show the world what the in vitro technique had achieved. At the same time, he needed to protect Larkin and Ava's identities.

"Now is not the time," James said. "I'm still playing the long game, Pops." He chuckled to himself—his dad had drifted off to sleep again while he was talking.

Suddenly, the door opened and a little boy ran into the room, hurtling himself toward James Sr.'s legs and hugging them. "Grandpa! Grandpa! Happy birthday!" Jameson squealed. James

Sr. woke up as Jameson clambered into his lap and hugged him around his neck.

Aubrey walked in a few steps behind him. "I am so sorry we're late," she said to James Jr. "One of the other docs had a family emergency, so I had to cover his call for a few extra hours."

"We're just glad you were able to make it," James Jr. replied.

"Hi, Mr. Davis, and happy birthday," Aubrey said as she squeezed his hand. Jameson was covering his grandfather's head in kisses. James Jr. was thankful his son had already gotten his flu and COVID shots as he watched Jameson smother James Sr. with potential fomites of adoration.

Aubrey sat in the chair next to Jameson's grandfather.

"Welcome, welcome to you both. So good to see you," he said as Jameson finally settled in his lap.

James Jr. knew his father didn't really understand who Aubrey was; his father often thought she was a nursing home employee or a random visitor. James Jr. would gently correct him by saying she was a good friend and Jameson's mom, but his dad would forget by the next time he saw her. Aubrey told James Jr. it didn't bother her—she was happy he was able to have a relationship with his only grandchild. He was also the only grandparent Jameson knew.

After Ava was born and Larkin had offered to be Aubrey's surrogate, Aubrey had called Dr. Davis and requested that they meet to discuss altering her eggs as they had done with Larkin's. They met in his office, which was still as cluttered as it had been when Larkin first started working there over ten years ago.

"So, Dr. Abrams, you want to be a part of this experiment?" Dr. Davis asked.

"Please call me Aubrey."

"And please call me James."

"Thank you, James. You know I already *have* been a part of this, very intimately, with my best friend. Now I'd like to be involved on a more personal level."

"If you're certain, I would be happy to oblige."

"Yes. I'm certain. Absolutely. But there's more that I hope you'll oblige."

"Yes?"

"I would like you to be the donor . . . but also the father," Aubrey said. She quickly added, "There would be no financial obligation. And you would make the 'donation,' so to speak, just as Spencer had for Larkin. I would want you to be involved with our child as much or as little as you would like."

"Why me?" he inquired.

"I have been looking at hundreds of bios for potential sperm donors. I've been looking for someone intelligent with a kind heart and calm temperament. No matter how much I read, I can't really know any of them." She hesitated. "I feel we've had a unique perspective on getting to know each other over the last couple of years, more than any online profiles could reveal."

"This is quite true," James Davis Jr. said, then sat back in his chair. He'd dedicated his life to his research. He had been singularly focused on that and nothing more. He had little time for hobbies, vacations, or relationships. He was now fifty-nine years old, and he had achieved a major milestone in his promise to his mother and his father. Now, he could be a part of his own research and be a father as well.

He saw his parents' wedding photo on the shelf behind Aubrey. They had gotten pregnant when they were in their early thirties and had anticipated having decades to raise their son together. In reality, his mother had only had three weeks.

With a wistful smile, he replied, "It would be an honor."

CHAPTER 26

When the middle school bus stopped in front of her home, Ava noticed her mother's car in the driveway. She jumped off the bus and ran to the front door. "Mom! Mom! Are you home?" she called as she dropped her backpack inside and kicked off her sneakers.

"Hey! I'm here. What's up? Big day at school?" Larkin asked from the kitchen. She had come home from work early when a shipment of lab supplies had been delayed.

"It's about my friend Lorna. Is Dad here?"

"He's in his office working. Want me to get him?" Larkin started walking toward his office.

"No!" Ava replied emphatically. "I don't want him to know. It's girl stuff."

"Okay. Sure."

Ava led her mom to the couch and sat down next to her with a serious expression on her face. Ava moved her long hair out of her face and tucked several strands behind her ears and began to rattle off what had happened at school. "Lorna got up in math class today to do a problem on the board and she had blood on the back of her pants. The teacher noticed right away and took her to the office to call her mom. She told the class she thought Lorna didn't look well. I don't think anybody else noticed what happened. Her mom brought her some more clothes, and I saw her again at lunch. She told me she started her period."

"Oh . . . is Lorna okay?" Larkin asked when Ava took a breath.

"Yes. She doesn't think anyone really noticed either. Her mom packed supplies in her backpack, but Lorna said she had no idea she was going to start."

"Well, I'm glad no one noticed."

"I don't want that to happen to me at school. Do you know when I might start? Is there a way to tell? Lorna's not even twelve yet! You said you didn't start until you were almost thirteen."

"Most girls take after their mothers, so you shouldn't need to worry about that happening soon."

"Oh, good! I just don't want to be surprised like Lorna." Ava paused. "Why are you looking at me so weird like that?" Ava asked as she noticed her mother's furrowed brow.

"Ava," Larkin said. "I don't think you're going to need to worry about what happened to Lorna happening to you. Remember how your dad and I told you how you were made unique? That you're special?"

"Yeah, but all parents say that." She rolled her eyes.

"You really *were* made different, Ava. Outside, you look like every other little girl your age, but inside, you're different. We think that when you get older, you won't have any periods."

"Why wouldn't I have a period? Doesn't having periods mean that I can have babies later if I want to? Are you saying I can't have babies?"

"You should still be able to have babies, honey," Larkin tried to reassure her. "But I think we need to go and talk to Aubrey. She can help with a lot of your questions."

A few days later, Larkin brought Ava to Aubrey's office at the end of her workday. They sat in her office as she finished with her last patient in an exam room. On her desk was a plastic model of a female human pelvis. It showed a cross section of a uterus with a full-term baby inside. Ava thought it was odd that the baby was upside down. When she hung upside down for too long from the monkey bars at school, it always made her head feel funny. She removed the baby from the uterus and tried to turn it the other way, but it wouldn't fit.

"Was Maeve upside down inside you?" Ava asked Larkin.

"Yes, and you and Jameson were as well."

"Did it hurt Maeve's head when she came out?" Ava asked as she rubbed the top of the plastic baby's head.

"No, honey. It didn't hurt her."

"And how long was she alive?"

"Just a few hours."

"That's so sad," Ava said as she put the baby back into the model on the desk.

"It was, and it still is."

"Were you scared I would be born like Maeve?"

"Very, very scared. I didn't think I wanted to have another baby for a long time, but I'm so glad I changed my mind. Your dad is, too."

"Hey, guys!" Aubrey said as she walked into her office. She hugged Larkin and Ava and then took a seat. "So, Ava, do you know why you are here today?"

Ava told Aubrey about her friend starting her period. She also said her mother had told her she might not menstruate, but she didn't understand why. Larkin then explained—in the best way she could to an eleven-year-old—that when Ava was just a tiny egg, before she was even Ava, a procedure had been done to change how she might have a baby when she grew up. Today was the day they would see if the procedure had worked. Aubrey would perform an ultrasound to take a look.

Aubrey had another plastic model on her desk—a uterus with two ovaries. It looked like the picture Dr. Mills had drawn on the exam table paper years ago when she'd explained female anatomy to Larkin. She showed the model to Ava. "So, women have a uterus that looks like this," she said. "These two round things are where the little eggs are made. If a woman gets pregnant, the baby grows inside the uterus for about nine months and then she has the baby. But you should be different. Let's go and see, okay?"

Aubrey and Larkin took Ava into an exam room and had her lie down. "I promise this isn't going to hurt," Aubrey said. "It just helps me to see inside your belly." As she maneuvered the ultrasound transducer across Ava's lower abdomen, Aubrey could see a long, tubular structure where the uterus would normally be and a single ovary, just like an avian species would have. The tubular structure appeared to be an oviduct. She pointed it out to Larkin, and they nodded to each other and smiled. It had worked.

"All is well, Ava," Aubrey told her. "You are healthy, but you shouldn't have periods like other girls."

Ava was confused but relieved. After her friend had started her period at school, Ava was happy to know she wouldn't have to worry about that happening to her. She sat up after Aubrey wiped the gel off her. She didn't have any other questions for Aubrey and was ready to go home.

"Do you want to know how you might have a baby, Ava? If you decide someday that you want a baby?" Larkin asked.

"I guess so," Ava replied with a shrug.

"So," Larkin started to explain. She took a deep breath. "You should be able to make an egg like your Silkies. And then your baby would grow inside the egg, like a chick, instead of growing inside of you."

Ava laughed at the idea and shook her head. "Stop teasing me! That's silly, Mom. Babies grow in bellies."

"I'm serious, Ava."

Ava paused as she realized her mother wasn't teasing her. "That's just really weird," Ava said flatly.

"Someday, lots of other women may be able to do the same thing. You wouldn't be the only one. You would just be the first.

But that's a long time from now. And you know how the chickens can't make eggs without a lot of sunlight?"

"Yes?"

"We should start having you keep sunglasses on when you're outside for a long time, okay?"

"Why?"

"Because if you don't, you could start producing eggs now that you're getting closer to puberty. You won't have to wear sunglasses every time you're outside—only if you're out for hours at a time in bright light."

Ava looked at Larkin and Aubrey with her head cocked to the side. They weren't playing a trick on her. This was real.

"I know this is a lot to be telling you today, but it's important for you to know. We can always talk more about this anytime you want to, I promise," Larkin said with sincerity.

The relief she felt from learning she wouldn't have a period was short-lived as Ava tried to absorb the information her mother had just told her. She decided she didn't ever want to have a baby. Ever.

CHAPTER 27

The pineal gland, located behind a chicken's eyes, is sometimes referred to as the "third eye" of the hen. When stimulated by sunlight in the orange and red spectrum, this gland sends hormone signals to the ovary to stimulate egg production.
—eggedon.com

Ava set her soccer bag next to her locker in the training room. Her sophomore year of high school would start the following week, and she was excited to have made the varsity team. She would be playing in the right forward position. Her team had been meeting early in the morning to avoid the hottest hours of brutal August sun, but at least the humidity was blissfully low today. They would continue their strength and conditioning program and practice drills. At the end of the day, they would have their first friendly scrimmage of the season against another local high school team.

She laced up her grass-stained cleats, with dried mud on the soles, as she sat on the long wooden bench. Some of the other girls were practicing their foot skills as she got ready. When her friend Jordan tried to kick a ball back to a teammate, she slipped and landed on Ava's backpack. Ava heard a *crack* as Jordan fell, and they both winced at the noise.

"Oh, I don't know what that was, Ava, but I'm so sorry!" Jordan said as she hastily got up.

Ava unzipped her backpack and pulled out her sport sunglasses. They were now mangled, and both lenses were cracked. She had forgotten to put them back in their case after the last practice. Her teammates knew she had a sensitivity to sunlight and always needed to wear them.

"Oh, no! I'll buy you a new pair, okay?" Jordan promised.

"It's really fine. I have a couple of spares at home." Ava didn't have a spare pair with her, though. For the past few years, she had been resolute about always wearing her sunglasses when she was outside, as her parents unfailingly reminded her to do. But she couldn't go home to get another pair—she wasn't able to drive yet—and her mom and dad weren't at home to bring her an extra pair. If she sat out of practice, the coach would make her run extra laps the next day. She decided that just one day without her sunglasses wouldn't matter.

Her team headed out to the field to work out in the early morning sun. They did sprints, lateral lunges, and single-leg squats. They took frequent water breaks, at least once every thirty minutes, as the temperature was already creeping toward ninety and it was only nine o'clock. After their trainer told them they were done for the morning, Ava practiced corner kicks and shooting on goal with Jordan helping her. Then she and several others helped the coach touch up the painted lines on the field.

One of the older girls who could drive later drove them to a restaurant, where they ate lunch. They hung out in the outdoor patio area, talking about the rival team, before heading back for the late afternoon scrimmage. Ava was squinting in the afternoon sun as they talked, and she tried to shade her eyes with her hand.

Her mom picked her up after the scrimmage was over as the sun was starting to go down. Ava excitedly mentioned that she had scored one goal and had two assists. She was happy her team had played so well, and she thought they were going to have a good season. To avoid a lecture on responsibility, she didn't mention that her sunglasses had been broken that morning. When she got home, she put two more pairs in her backpack, both in their protective cases.

The day school started the following week, Ava kept feeling random pain in her lower abdomen. It had begun the week before but was becoming more noticeable. It wasn't even a pain, really—it just felt different. The sensation was so unfamiliar to her, but she wrote it off as nervousness due to the new school year.

When Ava noticed that she was starting to look and feel bloated, she realized what was happening and began to panic. But who could she tell? Her parents would probably freak out and yell at her. Her friends absolutely wouldn't understand. She wished it would go away, as her fifteen-year-old mind reasoned was a possibility, and ignored it. Her soccer jersey was large and loose enough that no one noticed at practice, but she had to roll the waistline of her shorts down below her swollen midriff. She wore oversize T-shirts at school to hide her rapidly growing belly.

She was at her locker grabbing some markers for her art class when a classmate, Graham, opened the locker next to hers. She was rummaging around for an errant marker that had fallen to the bottom while absentmindedly balancing her spiral-bound sketchbook, using her distended abdomen like a shelf as she secured the book under her chin.

"Hey, Ava. Do you need some help holding things?" Graham offered.

She was startled, and as she looked up, her sketchbook fell to the floor.

"I got it," Graham said. He grabbed it and handed it to her with a grin that highlighted his dimples.

"Thank you so much!"

"Do you need any more help?"

"No, thanks, Graham," Ava replied, holding the book below her chest and over her stomach. She then pulled her backpack from over her shoulder and awkwardly held it in front of her. She tried to read his expression for clues as to what he was thinking, but he just seemed like his usual kind self.

"Okay, then. See ya later." He gave her a little salute as he headed to his class.

Graham had always been nice to her, but he was also nice to everyone. She didn't know anyone who disliked him. Teachers, coaches, classmates—no one had anything negative to say about him. She remembered that one of their homeroom teachers had called him "a good egg" one day. Ava had never heard that expression before, but once she learned what the phrase meant, she thought it was sweet and described him well.

He and Ava were in different social circles at school, so they never hung out together. But their lockers were next to each other because they were assigned based on alphabetical order, and they'd shared the same homeroom in middle and high school. For years, she'd spent the first ten minutes of her school day sitting at her desk, looking at the auburn hair on the back of his head, and listening to him talk and joke with his friends before the bell rang and they headed for their classes. She then saw him sporadically during the day, either in class or at their lockers. They rode on the same bus as he didn't live far from her, and they occasionally sat next to each other.

If he was absent from school, she missed the familiarity of his presence, and he seemed to feel the same way. When she'd had the flu and been out for a whole week during seventh grade, he'd welcomed her back with a quick hug and said he'd missed his locker buddy. But that was the sum of their relationship: They were friendly acquaintances by alphabetical happenstance.

Another week of school passed, and Ava sat on her bed typing an English essay on her laptop. It was based on her required summer reading, *To Kill a Mockingbird*. Her topic was the destruction of Scout's innocence as she developed a greater awareness of the pain and suffering in the world around her. As she wrote, she started to feel an overwhelming urge, as if she needed to have a bowel movement. Again, she knew why this was happening, and she now knew her desperate wishing had failed.

She stood and paced her bedroom's carpeted floor. Her parents wouldn't be home for a few more hours. She grabbed two towels from her bathroom, pulled her plush purple beanbag chair to the middle of the room, and made an indentation in the center. She laid the towels on top. Suddenly, she felt she had to push. She quickly pulled down her pants and squatted over the makeshift nest. Her eyes watered, and she felt her face flush.

Ava bore down and started pushing. She cried out as she felt something coming out of her, and she started sweating profusely. She continued to push as hard as she could while making deep, guttural noises. She finally felt a sense of relief when she had completely expelled the inanimate intruder from her body. It felt like an hour had passed, but it all occurred in a matter of minutes.

She pulled up her pants and underwear, sat down on the floor, and scooted away from the beanbag. Ava leaned against her bookcase, breathing heavily, her forehead beaded with sweat. She stared in silence and awe at the large peach-colored egg that sat in front of her in the hastily made accommodations. It was tinged with a small amount of blood.

"Peach. My bloom is peach. Just like my earlobes," she said with wonder as she absentmindedly rubbed her gold stud earrings.

"I made that. Oh, my God. I made an egg," she said in disbelief. "I am a freak of nature." She started to sob.

When she stopped crying, she wiped the tears from her face and stood to stare at what she had created in just a few weeks and laid within minutes. She carefully dragged the beanbag into her closet and closed the door, then tried to focus on her assignment while she waited for her parents to get home.

A few hours later, shortly after arriving home, her mom popped her head into Ava's room to say hi and let her know their dinner plans.

Ava nodded, said a quick "thanks" without taking her eyes off of her work, and went back to writing: *As Scout is introduced to more and more hard truths about the world, she loses her childhood innocence. That innocence later transforms into understanding.*

A while later, her mother called Ava to the dinner table. Her parents talked about events at work, but they were unsuccessful at prodding Ava to talk about school. Without looking at them, she gave vague answers to their questions and pushed the food around on her plate, taking only a few bites.

"You don't seem like yourself. Are you feeling bad, Avacado?" her father inquired.

"Yes, you have been very quiet. Did something happen today?" her mother asked with a look of concern.

"No, I'm not feeling fine, and yes, something happened," Ava mumbled. She stared down at her dinner plate and said nothing more.

"Ava, it will be okay, whatever it is," her father reassured her.

"It will have to be okay. I don't have a choice," Ava said as she pushed her chair back and got up from the table. She walked to her room and sat on her bed with her head buried in her bent knees. Her parents worriedly followed behind her.

Ava looked up at her mom and dad and said, "I just want to know why. *Why* did you do this to me?"

"Do what, honey?" her mother asked, confused. She looked at Ava's father.

Ava stared down at her feet and pointed to her closet.

"In there. Look in there."

Ava's parents walked over and opened the door. They looked down and saw the large egg nestled on the floor next to Ava's old stuffed animals and a stack of board games. Her mother gasped and covered her mouth, then stepped back and sat on the bed next to Ava. Her father kneeled to get a closer look.

"Oh, Ava. Are you hurting? Are you okay?" her mother asked as she touched her daughter's shoulder.

"Am I okay? Am I *okay*? No! I'm not okay!" Ava yelled as she pulled away from her mother.

"You did this to me. You both did this to me. No one asked me if I wanted this. You decided for me," she said with tears in her eyes.

"Yes, we did," her mother said. "You're right. We really felt this was the right decision to make for you. We wanted you to have more choices and control over your body than I did, but to do that, we had to make this choice for you first. We had no way to ask you before we made the decision."

"Our hope was that you would never have to experience what your mom did with Maeve," her father said. "Or what so many other women are experiencing now."

"And we're so sorry you were here alone when this happened, Ava," her mother added sincerely.

"I just feel like such a freak. This isn't . . . *normal*," Ava asserted.

"You're right—it isn't normal for people," her mother said. "But it *is* normal for other animals, and someday, it might be more normal for a lot of women. You are the proof that it works, and you're proof of what can be true for more women. This isn't how I wanted it to happen. I didn't want you to be surprised like this at your age, but this is incredible, Ava. This is amazing. It is life-changing." There was excitement in her mother's voice.

"I didn't want my life changed like this. I didn't ask for this." Ava cried as she told her parents about her sunglasses breaking and how she'd thought she would be okay for just one day. She hadn't really believed this could happen, but now she knew that's all it took. Just one day in the sun.

"Now you know, and we know, Ava," her father said. "It won't ever happen again. We will make sure your eyes are always protected. We'll do whatever it takes," he reassured her as Ava's mother continued to marvel at her creation.

"You don't need to help me," Ava said. "I know I won't ever make that mistake again. But what are we going to do with that?" She waved her hand toward the closet, and tears streamed down her face. "I want it gone. I don't want to look at it anymore. Please, just get rid of it," Ava urged.

A while later, Ava's parents led Dr. Davis to Ava's bedroom, where she was sitting in bed under her blanket, knees to her chest, proofreading her completed essay.

"Ava, Dr. Davis is here. Can we come in?" Ava's mother asked as she knocked.

"Sure," Ava replied flatly, refusing to look up.

Dr. Davis sat on the edge of her bed and apologized. "I am very sorry today was difficult for you, Ava. You may not know it now, but you are a hero, and you will be a legend. I may have been the innovator, and your mother was the courageous volunteer. But you . . . you are the one who is really going to make a difference in the world. You are living proof of what is attainable, and I thank you. And my parents, rest their souls, thank you."

Ava looked at Dr. Davis, whose expression was one of pure sincerity and gratitude. In a voice that was barely a whisper, she replied, "You're welcome."

He and her father gently lifted the egg and placed it in a large Styrofoam box lined with bubble wrap. Ava could tell that it wasn't very heavy, but they were both nervous about breaking it. Her mother placed the lid on top and looked up at Dr. Davis with a smile. He told them he would take it to the lab and store it in the refrigerator while he decided what to do next.

"It's time to let the world know what's possible," he said.

CHAPTER 28

La science n'a pas de patrie, parce que le savoir est le patrimoine de l'humanité.
—Louis Pasteur

A few weeks after Ava laid her egg, the Society of Genetics and Perinatal Medicine's annual conference was held in Chicago. There were about three hundred graduate students, research associates, physicians, and PhDs in attendance. The organization's president, Dr. Diya Singh, stepped up to the podium in the grand ballroom of the hotel where the meeting was being held. She announced to the audience, "Distinguished colleagues, you'll note on your programs that Dr. James Davis Jr. was added as a speaker at the last minute. We apologize for not having a printed handout prepared for his presentation, but he will provide a copy prior to your departure. And now, I would like to welcome Dr. Davis to the stage to present his most recent work."

Dr. Davis approached the dais to the attendees' applause as he shook Dr. Singh's hand. He then addressed the group.

"Thank you all. For those of you who are not familiar with me, my research over several decades has focused on facial morphogenesis and osteogenesis, and I've valued the professional collaborations I've had with many of you over the years. Your expertise and input have been invaluable. Today, however, I would like to discuss the research I have been pursuing in tandem. It is wholly unrelated to my usual area of study, and I'm pleased to present today a recent significant breakthrough." He then began his slide presentation, which was titled "An Alternate Evolutionary Pathway for Female Reproductive Development."

"As you know," he said, "there are three different ways in which mammals give birth. There are placental mammals, such as humans; marsupial mammals, such as kangaroos; and monotreme mammals, such as the platypus."

He paused before continuing. "I theorized that if humans were able to lay eggs, much like a monotreme or avian species, we could greatly decrease the rate of maternal morbidity and mortality that are inherent risks to childbearing. Therefore, my research has been on altering the human genome by splicing the genetic code for the human female's internal reproductive organs and replacing it with the code for the avian system."

Dr. Davis then went through his presentation slides, discussing how he'd achieved this goal by using an in vitro model, which led to subsequently developing an in vivo method using an intramuscular injection. Although his in vivo method had yet to be tested, he had achieved success with the in vitro model after finding a volunteer. This revelation was met with murmurs among the audience members—they undoubtedly knew that Dr. Davis's research hadn't been approved by an ethicist from any governing body.

"Yes, I know. You have postulated that my methods are unconventional, and you would be correct, but let's move on to the results for now. We can save those discussions for another time."

He then showed fluorescent microscopy photos of Larkin's embryos, one of which would someday be Ava. He simply referred to Larkin as "AV" for "anonymous volunteer" and the embryo as "Exhibit 1." He pointed to the areas on the Exhibit 1 chromosomes that had been spliced and replaced.

He then showed the ultrasound photos Aubrey had taken of Ava's internal reproductive organs—the prepubescent Exhibit 1—highlighting the single ovary and long, tubular oviduct. This was met with scoffs from the audience. The photos proved nothing as they could have come from an internet search for the reproductive system of any random bird.

Dr. Davis embraced the skepticism. "There was a reason I have waited this long to present my findings," he said. "I needed to protect the identities of the persons involved, and I needed definitive proof that this procedure had succeeded, which is precisely why I am here now." He signaled for Susan to join him on the dais.

She had been seated next to a large cooler, which she wheeled onto the stage. From it, she removed a large item wrapped in several layers of gauze and placed the bundle on a raised platform. She and Dr. Davis carefully unwrapped the object as the crowd looked on in quiet anticipation.

They revealed to the audience a large egg, at least twice as large as what an ostrich would produce. The onlookers were doubtful. A few laughed derisively, but Dr. Davis reassured them that the egg was indeed real and unfertilized. He then showed them slides of the chromosomal and DNA analysis of a sample he'd removed from the egg using a small diamond-point drill bit to extract some of the albumen. The findings were almost 99 percent consistent with human DNA, save for the section of the code that had been altered.

He encouraged audience members to come onto the stage a few at a time for a closer look. He also offered to let them take samples from the egg's albumen or a small portion of the shell to their own labs for independent testing. Many requested samples, and he obliged by drilling another small hole as Susan helped them retrieve the contents. She also helped them cut small pieces of the shell to take with them for analysis.

Although there were many doubters who were convinced this was nothing more than an elaborate hoax, several of those in attendance were gradually swayed. They knew how brilliant Dr. Davis was, and they were convinced that he had succeeded. Women could lay eggs with this new technology. His methods were neither ethical nor conventional, but the results were incredible.

Social media quickly became inundated with photos and videos from the conference, and within hours, Dr. Davis's presentation was the top trending news story. Some thought it was simply a joke and scrolled past. Some thought it was just another random, ridiculous conspiracy. But two groups were paying close attention: the US government and many, many women of reproductive age. Women without access to birth control except through unlawful means. Women who were desperate, seeking illegal abortions, and suffering the consequences of complications. Women who wanted more options for their daughters than the law allowed.

Several news agencies contacted Dr. Davis for interviews in the days after the conference. He was pleased to have a larger audience so he could clear up any misconceptions.

"Please tell us, Dr. Davis, would women lay eggs every day? Every few weeks?" one journalist, Nicole Darcy, asked on her prime-time news program.

"No, not at all," he said. "Like hens, women would need to be exposed to many hours of sunlight per day to produce an egg. Wearing sunglasses that block a significant amount of light in the orange and red spectrum should serve as adequate prevention against ovulation. When a woman is ready to procreate, she would simply remove her eye protection and make sure she gets an adequate amount of sunlight, likely twelve to fourteen hours a day."

"So, just sunglasses? That's the new contraception? No hormones?"

"Correct. So that would be another upside for women. No complications from taking a pill or getting a hormone shot or an IUD. No weight gain, no risk of blood clots."

"Which is a moot point in our country right now."

"Yes, that is true."

"But it would be really difficult for the government to ban aviators, wouldn't it?" the interviewer mused.

"I believe that would be impractical."

"And women would no longer have periods?"

"That is correct. No periods. No more feminine hygiene products would be needed. So this has practical cost and environmental benefits as well."

"And the actual reproductive process will remain unchanged?"

"Sexual intercourse will not be affected, correct. But hopefully it'll be more enjoyable when people are able to plan a family more easily and not worry about unplanned pregnancies."

"And how long will it take for a woman to produce an egg?"

"From my limited knowledge, as only one egg has been produced so far, it appears to be less than three weeks."

"And what would be the gestation period?"

"Well, the correct term now would be 'incubation,' not 'gestation.' That is undetermined at this time as we do not have a fertilized egg to study, but I suspect it would be similar to the current gestation period. When the neonate is fully developed, the shell would have to be removed, as humans lack the egg tooth that birds, reptiles, and monotremes have to hatch themselves."

"And will a woman have to sit on the egg for nine months? Or will she have to talk an elephant into doing it so she can take a proper vacation to Palm Beach?" The interviewer laughed at her own joke.

"Aha! My son loved that book when he was a toddler. No, no. I am working on designing an incubator like the ones used for the chicken eggs in my lab, but on a larger scale."

Nicole's tone became more serious. "You may not be aware, Dr. Davis, but I nearly died several years ago from an untreated ectopic pregnancy when I was living in Texas. I nearly hemorrhaged to death because my doctor feared being jailed for giving me lifesaving care."

"Yes, I remember the news story. I'm very sorry that happened to you, and it was very brave of you to share your experience."

"Unfortunately, bravery doesn't change laws," Nicole said as she turned toward the camera. She then shifted back to Dr. Davis. "So, I would like to know. Would women who can lay eggs never experience an ectopic pregnancy?"

"Chickens may experience something similar. It's called an egg yolk coelomitis. This is more common in commercial egg-laying breeds, so this may be an effect on the reproductive tract that occurs from frequent laying. Hopefully, it will not happen in their human counterparts."

"So, egg laying still has inherent risks?"

"Yes. It's not perfect, but it's a vast improvement to traditional pregnancy and childbirth, in my opinion."

"And what about abortion, Dr. Davis? What do you envision that will look like in the future if more women agree to be guinea pigs—or, rather, guinea hens?"

"Very clever," he replied with a smile. "Well, my hope is that it would be unnecessary. With proper eye protection, there would be no unplanned fertilizations."

"But what if there were? What then?"

"Well, if the egg isn't incubated, it simply won't grow. Or, if a woman chooses adoption, someone else could incubate her egg and the baby could be adopted. But my hope is that ophthalmologists will develop specialized contacts to help prevent any unplanned events. A good pair of sunglasses currently filters 75 to 90 percent of orange and red light, but I would prefer glasses and contacts that provide 100 percent protection to be safe."

"And what do you say to critics who say you are playing God, Dr. Davis?"

"I'd say God gave us knowledge for medical advances to improve the quality of life and save lives. And that is my intent—to save lives, not to play God."

CHAPTER 29

The Farm to Table in St. Louis seats about 80–100 guests, I believe. Their omelets are absolutely divine. Planning to go next Tuesday first thing when they open!

I think the same family has a place in Atlanta that seats at least 120. May go Friday. Very excited.

Sitting in her home office, Larkin used her laptop to read coded comments in the social media group Aubrey had created: Ob-Gyns for Farm to Table Fandom. Using Aubrey's account to keep her own identity anonymous, Larkin replied to them by saying *Sounds like fun* or *Will have to check it out.*

While Dr. Davis was at the meeting, Aubrey and Larkin had moved the thousands of injections he'd prepared and stored in his lab to a storage unit near Aubrey's home. After Dr. Davis appeared on the national news, Aubrey had spread the word to colleagues who'd had enough of their hands being tied by the courts making medical decisions for pregnant women. They joined the social media site if any of their patients were interested in getting the injection and mentioned the desired quantity on the Fandom page, along with the city where the injections should be delivered. The underground group transported the injections and met at shuttered Planned Parenthood buildings in various cities for distribution using an operation similar to the one they already used to distribute black-market birth control.

The shot was untested and unvetted, but women clamored for the opportunity to change their future children's lives. They didn't foresee any governmental changes or constitutional protections in the near future. They had only seen decades of increasing restrictions and a government that had successfully dominated through gerrymandering, voter suppression, and Supreme Court nominations. They'd tried peaceful protesting and they'd tried getting out the vote, but nothing had changed. Now they had hope.

Larkin was jotting down quantities and cities when Ava came in.

"Mom?"

"Yeah, honey?" Larkin replied and turned around in her chair.

"Can I talk to you?"

"Of course. What's up?"

Ava said down on the ottoman across from Larkin.

"I saw a clip of Dr. Davis's interview. Is anyone going to find out who I am?"

"No. I promise. Your name hasn't been associated with anything. No one will know. We'll protect your identity."

"But don't they have my DNA now? Those other scientists took samples of my egg. Aren't there databases? Like when people want to find their ancestors? Can't they just plug it in and figure out who I am?" Ava's voice shook as she spoke. "Will we go to jail? Or will they lock me up in a lab cage somewhere?"

Sensing Ava's distress, Larkin tried to calm her. She said, "Ava, the scientists aren't interested in revealing your identity. They only want to verify that this is possible . . . that women can lay eggs. No one wants to 'out' you. This is purely science."

"They might not want to, but other people might. They would want to put the freak on trial or try an exorcism or something."

"Please don't worry," Larkin begged her daughter.

"Don't worry? The President of the United States called me an abomination, Mom." Ava stood and started pacing the room.

"And an affront to God. Lots of people agree with him. They want to know who I am. We just learned about the Salem Witch Trials in school. It's scaring me."

"I promise I won't let anything happen to you." Larkin stood and reached her hand out to Ava.

Larkin watched as Ava's face turned red with anger and she refused to take her mother's hand. "Do you even hear what you're saying, Mom? You already let something happen to me. All of this is because *you* let something happen to *me*." Ava pointed to her mother and then herself for emphasis as she spoke. "I'm now scared because of the decision you made for me. My life has changed because of *your* decision, not mine." Ava stepped over to Larkin's desk. "And now you're helping other moms do this to their kids?" Ava gestured to the laptop. "I don't think Maeve was the only one whose brain didn't develop," Ava muttered and regarded her mother.

Larkin was taken aback by her daughter's callous comment. She recognized the fear and hurt on Ava's face, the same face she'd instantly fallen in love with when Ava was born. Larkin had felt a surge of endorphins wash over her at the moment of her daughter's birth. It had felt like the closest thing she could imagine to pure happiness. In that moment, she had felt a love for Ava that was so strong it hurt her heart, and she would do anything to protect her.

"Oh, God, Ava. I understand why you're upset." Larkin remained still, afraid Ava would leave before she was able to explain. "I am so sorry. I promise, I did this for you. To help you. To not have to go through what I did with Maeve." Ava started to walk out of the office, but Larkin implored, "Ava, please, please listen."

Ava stopped in the doorway with her back turned to her mother.

Larkin continued. "When I learned Maeve had no chance of living and I was told I couldn't have an abortion, every day leading up to her birth was mentally torturous. I didn't think I could handle knowing she was growing inside me every day, only to be forced to watch her die." Ava remained facing the door as Larkin added, "And I was right. I didn't handle it well at all. I didn't understand why it was so important to other people for Maeve to die when they decided it was acceptable for her to die." She stopped and cleared her throat. "I wanted to die with her rather than experience pregnancy and childbirth. I never told your dad, but every single day before she was born, I thought of how I could kill myself as some sort of apology to her because I failed her." Larkin stammered as she recounted the memory. "First, I thought my body failed somehow by not giving her a brain, and then I thought I was failing to give her what I truly felt was a less tragic end to her life." Larkin watched as Ava lowered her head down and her posture softened.

"And then Dr. Davis told me about his work. I wanted this for you, and he wanted it for me and more women. And I agreed. I am so very sorry. I didn't think about how it would truly impact you, but I promise, I did this to protect you and others from experiencing what I did."

Ava turned around and embraced Larkin so hard that Larkin could barely breathe. Larkin felt the familiar rush of endorphins again.

"I didn't know you wanted to die, Mom. I'm so glad you're here. I didn't know how awful it was. I'm so, so sorry that happened to you. And I'm so sorry about Maeve, and what I said. I'm just so scared." Ava buried her face in Larkin's shoulder and sobbed.

"My sweet Avacado," Larkin murmured into Ava's hair as she gently rubbed her daughter's back. "I'll do everything I can to keep you anonymous. And you won't be alone in this forever. As we keep distributing these injections, there are going to be a lot more just like you someday."

CHAPTER 30

September 9, 2058
AP News
Federal government denounces "the Hen Party." Vows to shut down further research.

Dr. Davis returned to work after a frenetic week of television, magazine, and podcast interviews. Susan stopped him in the hallway as he walked toward the lab. She began frantically apologizing for what was happening. He walked into the room, where Larkin and two graduate students watched from a corner while authorities from the Food and Drug Administration unplugged hard drives and went through filing cabinets. Susan told him there were more of them in his office. The investigators didn't speak as they gathered information and boxed items to be taken away.

Dr. Davis welcomed them and sat down with his colleagues. He asked if the agents would like any coffee or snacks but received no response. He decided to get himself a cup of coffee and went up to his office, where the other FDA workers were.

"If I may be of assistance, I believe this would be of interest to you," he said, handing a ledger to one of the investigators. It contained detailed financial information showing how the money from his trust had been spent to fund his research. Every dollar was accounted for in the ledger, and he still had funds left over thanks to wise investments. He assured them that none of the research money he'd received from the federal government had been used for the Hen Project, as the media had nicknamed it. The government referred to those involved as the Hen Party, which amused Dr. Davis. It made it sound as if they were their own political organization, and it felt like a proper uprising to him. It was some of that good trouble his father had wanted.

"You are more than welcome to any of the information here," he said. "And please feel free to ask me any questions you may have."

Again, he received no response.

Dr. Davis knew the investigation would provide very little information other than what he had given them. He had been careful over the years to take notes using only paper and pen, and he'd shredded them when he was done with one phase and moved on to the next. There were no floppy disks from when he'd started the project, nor was any newer research stored in the cloud. The conversations he'd had with colleagues over the years had been conducted via landline only, and he'd never emailed anyone with follow-up questions. He'd been very careful to protect the identities of Aubrey, Larkin, Jameson, and Ava. And he told them Susan's only involvement had been helping to transport the egg to the meeting.

However, anyone who wanted to reproduce the final elements of his work was free to do so. At the conference, he'd provided the attendees with key information about his research, enabling the injections to be produced and duplicated on a massive scale. He'd also made the information available online. He wasn't exactly sure what more the investigators would want, but he let them rummage freely.

Dr. Davis sipped his coffee as he watched box after box being carried out of his office. Then he walked down to the lab, apologized for the chaos, and told the graduate students to go home. The FDA had left, and Larkin and Susan were cleaning and reorganizing. He could tell they both had been crying.

"Why the tears?" he asked. "It doesn't look too bad in here." He set down his mug and started moving the lab chairs back into place.

"We don't want you to get arrested and spend the rest of your life in jail," Susan replied with a tearstained face.

"Now, there's no need to worry about me. I've already lived the best of my life, and there's probably not too much left of the rest of my life, right? Ten years? Maybe twenty?" he said with a wide grin and outstretched arms. He put his hands on his hips and thought out loud. "Spencer is an actuary. I should ask him to estimate what life in prison would mean for a seventy-year-old man such as myself. My dad lived until ninety-two . . ."

As Larkin regarded her beloved mentor, she shook her head with bewilderment. Then she wiped her eyes and went back to putting the lab back in order.

He picked up his coffee and sat down to enjoy it, nonplussed.

Ultimately, Dr. Davis didn't serve any jail time. The FDA hadn't been able to complete its investigation because it couldn't determine the identities of the volunteer or Exhibit 1. Dr. Davis didn't even receive a fine since there was no law against privately funded germline human genome editing. After reviewing the financial records, the FDA confirmed that he had only used his own money. However, he was banned from receiving any further government research funding secondary to "ethical misconduct." He apologized to Susan and Larkin for having to shut down his lab.

They would not accept his apology. Susan was of retirement age, and she decided to spend her time fostering cats and kittens. Her husband was fully on board—he had accepted long ago that he would always be surrounded by cats. And Larkin told Dr.

Davis this was a great time for her to go back to college and pursue a graduate degree.

Despite no longer having his own laboratory, Dr. Davis stayed busy fielding calls from other researchers. A pharmaceutical lab in Canada began mass-producing the injections and planned to begin recruiting volunteers to perform appropriate clinical trials if their governing research agencies gave approval. Researchers were surprised by the amount of interest Canadian women showed in participating and who wanted to volunteer despite having access to contraception and abortion.

As Canadian scientists waited for approval to start their trials, demand for the injections in the United States continued. To prepare for the next generation of daughters, Dr. Davis began meeting with leaders in ophthalmology, engineering, and obstetrics.

In about ten or so years, there would be a demand for better eye protection to prevent unplanned ovulation in pubescent girls whose mothers had received the treatment. He also spoke to engineers about developing incubators for the eggs based on a design he'd made using the incubator in his lab as a prototype. It needed to have temperature and humidity control, turn the egg several times a day, and be sold at an affordable price. Finally, it needed a digital monitor that would attach to the egg and keep track of the growing baby's heart rate and movements, like those already available for chicken eggs.

Dr. Davis met with multiple obstetricians about their role in monitoring and assisting with the births. These professionals had no experience with this new type of delivery and were unsure how to monitor the embryo's growth and development. The obstetricians and midwives who'd be assisting with the deliveries would need specialized training, and they would have to learn in the moment.

He reassured them that they could monitor growth with ultrasounds by drilling a fenestration through the large part of the egg, filling the air cell with sterile saline, and placing the ultrasound transducer in this area. When the yolk was completely absorbed and the fetus occupied the entire egg, it would be time for delivery. He reassured them that the reduction of maternal and perinatal complications would be well worth the learning curve.

The government instituted a swift response to Dr. Davis's research. The current President of the United States, who had been Jack Montogomery's vice president, issued an executive order banning further human genome editing using germline cells (the cells that form eggs in females and sperm in males). His original plan of banning all human gene editing was met with opposition from his own party, as this would have halted advances in almost all aspects of medicine, including oncology, autoimmune disorders, and infectious diseases.

Then, all anyone could do was wait. Wait for Exhibit 1, now referred to simply as X1, to reveal herself, and wait to see if she would produce more eggs. Media interest slowly waned over the years when no new news developed. Chat room theorists concluded that she wasn't real and anyone who still believed she existed was foolish. Some theorized that X1 had died of complications from the untested genetic manipulation. There was further speculation that Dr. Davis was simply a shill for women's activists, he was just trying to make a point, and X1 had never existed.

CHAPTER 31

When Ava and Graham graduated from high school, the days of seeing each other almost daily ended abruptly, and they left for college in different cities a few months later. When she completed college, Ava started teaching at an elementary school in her hometown. She heard from her parents that Graham and several of his friends were opening a pub in town. She also learned that Graham had earned a degree in brewing science while studying in North Carolina and he would be the pub's master brewer.

She and a group of coworkers decided to check out the new local brewery on opening night. She sat with her friends at a corner table, and she recognized Graham immediately. He was busy delivering beer flights to customers and answering their questions about the brewing process, the alcohol content by volume for each of the beers, and where he'd learned his craft. He also discussed their selection of pilsners, ales, IPAs, and lagers.

When he came to Ava's table, her friends each ordered a flight of the lighter beers. But Ava preferred the darker beers and asked about the selection of porters and stouts. Graham's eyes lit up when he saw her.

"Ava! My old locker buddy! How the hell are you?" He leaned in to give her a hug.

"Great! So good to see you, and congratulations on your business! I know you're slammed right now. Maybe we can catch up later."

"That'd be great!"

Ava enjoyed listening to his calm, deep voice as he described each of the beverage selections in detail to everyone at the table, noting their differences. At the end of the night, after some malted barley and hops catalyzed her courage, she asked Graham out for a date, and he enthusiastically said yes.

Their first date was an early morning hike at a local state park. Towering tulip poplars shaded their path. As they talked, they realized how little they knew about each other despite their daily high school interactions. She was now a third-grade teacher who loved her job, and her students loved her energy. He'd originally wanted to teach chemistry but realized he could unite his love of chemistry and beer to form a career. Ava learned that he had two brothers and a sister. Then he asked Ava if she had siblings. She told him about Maeve and how she had died ten years before Ava was born.

They sat down on the rocks next to a small creek to drink from their water bottles, and Graham offered her some snacks from his backpack. When he asked her about Maeve, Ava told him she'd always wondered what it would have been like to grow up with an older sister and what Maeve would have been like if she had survived. Ava also told him how the experience had affected her parents and how they'd almost chosen not to have another child.

Graham said he was thankful they'd changed their minds. His smile always looked like a slight smirk, and Ava had no idea what else he was thinking but not saying.

"Can I ask you something that I've wondered about since tenth grade?" Graham inquired in between bites of his protein bar.

"Tenth grade? When my team beat you in the Mathletes competition? Are you still feeling dejected about your humiliating loss?" she teased.

"Ha! I forgot about that. That does bring up some painful memories, but no . . . that's not it." He paused and shook his head, deciding to say nothing more.

"I really don't mind you asking me anything."

"Are you sure?"

Ava nodded reassuringly.

"Okay . . . well . . . so . . . were you ever pregnant in high school?"

Ava looked at him with surprise and chuckled. "Oh! No! That's funny. Was someone saying I was? The only reputation I thought I had was for being a nerd."

"No, no one . . . I just noticed at the lockers one time at the beginning of tenth grade . . . you looked like you were very pregnant and trying to hide it. And then, a week later, you were back to normal. I thought I was losing my mind. I wondered if you'd had a baby over the weekend and your parents made you place the baby for adoption. I had invented this whole scenario in my head about you having a secret baby."

"Oh . . . did you tell anyone about that?"

"No. I would never have done that to you." He shook his head emphatically.

"Well, thank you. And I really wasn't pregnant, but you weren't losing your mind." Ava hesitated.

"If I can ask you anything, then you can trust me with anything," he said with genuineness.

Ava looked at Graham and saw only kindness in his brown eyes. She longed to confide in someone, but she had never trusted anyone with her story. But learning he had kept her high school "pregnancy" secret for years, she sensed he could keep her true secret as well.

"Do you remember all the news stories about the Hen Project about eight years ago? During the fall of our sophomore year in high school? And the media was trying to identify X1, the woman who supposedly had avian reproductive organs and laid an egg?" Ava asked him.

"Yes. My parents thought it was just some CGI hoax when they saw the egg and—"

Ava interrupted him. "It wasn't a hoax."

The realization quickly came over him. "It's you, Ava? You're X1?"

Ava nodded.

"Please, please don't tell anyone," she begged. "There are only six other people who know. I never told any of my friends. I didn't wear eye protection the summer before tenth grade, and that's when we realized what I could do. I was so scared when it happened. That was when you thought I was pregnant. But I wasn't 'with child,' I was 'with egg.'" She laughed softly at her own joke and tossed a rock into the stream.

He stared at her in astonishment.

"This is why I never told anyone," Ava said flatly. "Your face says it all. I am a mutant."

Graham burst out in laughter and hugged her tightly. Then he held her by her shoulders and looked into her eyes.

"Ava, you are not a mutant. You're just Ava to me. This changes nothing."

After their hike, they went to their own homes to clean up before meeting again for dinner that night.

When Ava got out of the shower and wrapped up in her towel, she heard her phone ding. She glanced down at her phone on the bathroom counter. Graham had texted: *I think you are seggsy*.

Ava laughed out loud.

Then there was another message. She picked up her phone and read, *Much more importantly, I think you are smart, kind, beautiful, and unique. There truly is no one else like you.* She held her phone to her heart and grinned.

She was towel-drying her hair when she heard another ding. She glanced at the new text message: *You're perfect, Ava.*

Graham and Ava married a few years later, and they rented a home while they saved money to buy their own place. Emery, Ava's friend and a teacher who worked with her at the elementary school nearby, was renting the house's second bedroom while she waited to get married in six months.

"Ava! Hey, Ava!" Emery called to her roommate as she knocked on Ava's bedroom door one morning before work.

Graham opened the door with his eyes half closed. He yawned as he asked, "What's up, Emery?"

"I'm so sorry to wake you! Is Ava still here?" Emery peered past him and saw a lump of comforter on the bed with Ava's feet poking out from the bottom.

"I'm here. Getting up soon," Ava mumbled into her pillow.

"Do you mind if I look in your bathroom cabinet for a tampon? I'm out," Emery asked.

"Help yourself," Graham replied as he flopped back into bed next to Ava.

Emery went into their bathroom and opened the cabinet under the sink. She moved bottles of hair care products and rolls of toilet paper to the side until she found a box of tampons in the very back. The box was still in its original plastic wrap and dusty on top. She opened it and grabbed a few.

Ava sat up in bed, rubbing the sleep out of her eyes.

Emery came out of the bathroom with a sheepish expression on her face. She held up some tampons and thanked her friend. "My period came early this month, so I had to grab some from you. So happy you had some! I'll buy you some more, okay?"

"Oh . . . don't worry about it. I don't use them."

"Looking at the box, I figured you might not. They look like they've been sitting there for years!"

Ava stammered as she recalled the box of tampons she kept in case her friends ever needed one. "Um . . . yeah. I use a menstrual cup. I just have those for emergencies."

"I never could get used to the cup. You are a much better friend to Mother Gaia than I am. Thank you for having these!" Emery exited their bedroom and closed the door.

Graham reached his arm out to Ava and beckoned her to lie down a little longer with him. She snuggled next to him, and he wrapped his arm around her waist. She could feel his warm breath on her neck. She gently stroked the hair on his arms, which were covered in freckles. His hands were rough and calloused from hauling containers of hops to the storage freezer and opening beer bottles by hand rather than searching for an opener.

She kissed every callus and rolled out of bed to get ready for work. Then she called out to Emery, offering to carpool. That afternoon, as they rode together in Ava's car, Ava asked Emery how her wedding plans were going.

"Really great! We have the church and the reception venue so far. My mom and I are going to Nashville to look for wedding dresses next weekend."

"That's exciting, Emery! Graham and I are looking forward to the wedding."

"I'm so glad! I hope it's fun for everyone. I'm nervous about the wedding night, though, and it's still months away."

Ava knew Emery and her fiancé had taken a purity vow and promised to remain abstinent before they married, in keeping with their religious beliefs. There had been a direct relationship between the contraception bans and strengthened abortion restrictions and an increase in young adults choosing abstinence either out of pietism, fear of pregnancy, or a combination of the two.

"I'm sure it will be fine," Ava reassured her. "Are you worried about the actual sex or getting pregnant?"

"The sex. My mom hasn't really talked to me about it, and my other close friends have also taken purity vows, so they don't know what to expect either. I just don't want it to hurt. But I'm not worried about getting pregnant. Why would I be?"

"Do you want a baby right away?"

"If I get pregnant, then it was meant to be. We won't interfere with God's plan," Emery replied and then added, "I really hope you and Graham aren't using any contraception. It's illegal, you know. I've just tried my best to love the sinner, but not the sin. Know what I mean?"

Yeah, you just called me a sinner, Ava thought but didn't reply. Instead, she focused on driving.

"I know you don't feel the same way, Ava. And that's fine, but more and more people think like me. We agree with the direction of our country."

"Yep. I don't agree. Not a bit." Ava started biting the inside of her cheek to distract herself from the conversation.

"We have been so thankful for the leadership we've had over the last several decades. People who share my beliefs had to live with *Roe v. Wade* for fifty years when we knew how wrong it was, and we're relieved with where we are now. We are saving babies' lives. We won't let that change," Emery stated with an air of certainty.

Ava didn't take her eyes off the road as she replied. "But why can't you and those like you practice abstinence and not use contraception and let the rest of us do what is right for us and our beliefs? I don't care what you do in your bedroom. Why do you care about what I do?" She gripped the steering wheel tightly as she braced herself for Emery's reply.

"Because it's not just about *my* babies. It's about saving all human lives. We aren't being selfish. We're being servants of God."

"So, I'm a selfish baby killer if I use contraception and plan for a family?"

"Yes, Ava," Emery stated firmly. "The pill, Depo, IUDs. All those are preimplantation chemical abortions, and I hope they're never legal again. They all change the lining of the uterus so an embryo . . . *a human life* . . . can't implant and *dies*. The end result is the same as an abortion. No difference."

Ava pulled into their driveway and looked at her friend. "That's not at all how hormonal contraception works, Emery. *At all*. Now I'm afraid to know how you think sex works. Jesus. I hope you know you have three holes down there. I hope your fiancé finds the right one. Godspeed to you on your wedding night." She sighed with exasperation and got out of the car.

"You don't need to come to my wedding anymore, Ava," Emery huffed as Ava slammed the car door.

A few weeks later, Emery moved in with her parents.

CHAPTER 32

Emerald Isle, North Carolina, was a favorite vacation spot for Graham and Ava. His family had owned a beach house there for many years, and they visited at least once a week every summer. They usually vacationed with his family, but they went alone to celebrate their first anniversary.

Ava breathed in the sweet scent of coconut as Graham gently massaged sunscreen into her back, the warmth of the sun mingling with the cool, soothing touch of his hands. They sat in beach chairs under a broad umbrella planted firmly in the sand. A gentle, refreshing breeze danced across the beach, carrying with it the quiet hum of the ocean. It was the kind of day made for doing nothing—just the rhythmic sound of waves and the shared comfort of their company. They'd agreed, in the spirit of their getaway, to leave behind the chatter of the pub and the demands of teaching, allowing themselves this rare, perfect pause from the world.

Ava slipped off her sunglasses and tucked them into her beach bag. She removed the novel she'd just begun from the side pocket, then slid her chair out from beneath the umbrella, reclining it halfway. She glanced at her husband, offering him a smile, before opening her book and sinking comfortably back into her chair, letting the warm sunlight wash over her.

Just one day in the sun. That's all I need, Ava thought.

Midway through their weeklong vacation, Ava was sunning in her chair again, reading the rest of her book. She started having a familiar sensation in her abdomen, one that she'd had more than ten years ago when she was in high school. This time it brought her excitement rather than dread.

She reached over and grabbed Graham's hand. "I think we are going to have a baby."

"That fast? You can tell?"

"Yes," she nodded. "I'm pretty sure."

He gave her hand a squeeze and laughed. "Well, that is fan-fucking-tastic!"

Just as it had happened before, Ava's abdomen quickly grew over the next two weeks. When they arrived home after their vacation, Graham went to their bedroom closet and took out the unique wedding gift Dr. Davis had given them. It was something that no other couple would have looked for or added to their registry—it was the egg incubator with the wooden exterior that had been in Dr. Davis's lab, the one Larkin and Susan had used many times. He'd modified the internal mechanism that had once housed several dozen eggs and redesigned it for one large egg.

Graham pushed it to the corner of their bedroom, plugged it in, and flipped the red switch on the side. The inside gears started to turn very slowly, like a relaxing Ferris wheel. They made a soft whirring noise as they moved. After a full cycle, the movement stopped. In an hour or so, it would begin turning in the opposite direction. It would repeat this process until it was turned off. He checked the temperature and humidity controls to make sure they were on the settings Dr. Davis had instructed them to use. The incubator was decades old but worked perfectly. Ava and Graham stood together, looking at the new gadget and listening to the tranquil white noise.

"Most couples get espresso machines and toasters for wedding gifts," Ava said with her head cocked to the side as she rested a hand on top of her stomach.

"But this is much, much cooler. And the sound is even better than the white noise of gentle rain or nature sounds. We are going to sleep like babies," Graham teased.

"Aren't you nervous at all?"

"Sure. No different than any new dad would be. You?"

"Yes . . . a little. At least I know sort of what to expect for the first part. It should be any day now."

Ava slept restlessly that night. When she woke up the next morning with a familiar feeling, she shook Graham's shoulder. "Graham. Graham . . . Graham! Wake up! It's time."

Graham sat up with a start. Ava got out of bed and gestured for him to come to her at the base of the bed. A few days earlier, they had fashioned a makeshift spot with layers of soft blankets, like the one she had hastily assembled as a teenager. She was wearing a short, thin nightgown and quickly removed her underwear, tossing them on the floor. She had Graham stand in front of her with his arms bent. She tightly held his forearms to brace herself as she squatted.

"Should I do anything else? Are you hurting?" Graham asked calmly.

"I'm fine . . . I'm fine. This is good. Stop talking. Thank you." Ava's voice was raspy as she put her head down to focus on breathing and bearing down.

Her breaths became more shallow and rapid as she steadied herself against Graham, and her grip on his wrists became stronger, draining the color from his hands. Her nails dug into his skin. When she looked up and saw him grimace, Ava was thankful she kept her nails trimmed. She made several short, soft grunts followed by one longer and louder grunt, and then she let out a long sigh of relief as her grip loosened. She stood shakily with Graham steadying her. He brushed the damp hair out of her face, and she gave him a slow, deep kiss before embracing him warmly.

Then she stepped to the side and they stared in silence at the perfect egg she'd made. It had the same peach bloom as the first.

"Oh, my God. That was amazing. *You* are amazing," Graham said in disbelief. His arm was wrapped around her waist.

"That was so much better than doing it alone," Ava said.

"What can I do? Here . . . lay down on the bed." Graham held her arm as he helped her to the bed and sat next to her. He turned on the heating pad, laid it on her stomach, and offered her a glass of water from the nightstand.

"I really feel fine. Definitely sore, but it's not awful. I just want you to get the egg in the incubator, please. I don't want it to get cold."

Graham scrambled out of bed with the sudden realization that he needed to take care of the egg. He picked it up with a soft towel and gently placed it into the incubator.

They sat in bed together, mesmerized as they watched the oval object turn and listened to the continuous hum of the machinery.

"And I thought that noise would help me sleep. I don't think I'll be able to sleep until it hatches," Graham said.

"Wow," Ava said. "This is the first time I've ever seen you nervous."

"Well, this is the first time I've ever seen my wife, or anyone, lay an egg, and that egg is going to nourish our child . . . our baby. I'm just a bit . . . what's the right word?" He paused and tapped his chin pensively, then looked into her eyes. In a serious tone, he said, "Shell-shocked." He looked at Ava with a self-satisfied grin as he leaned forward, pecked her on the forehead, and gave her an innocent expression.

"Already cracking the dad jokes, huh?" she said, grinning.

Spencer and Larkin came later that day to see their daughter's second egg. This time, they were able to share in Ava's happiness and disbelief.

They watched as the large egg housing their future grandchild turned slowly in the same incubator Larkin had used when she'd first started her job with Dr. Davis. Larkin commented that it was a little loud and old, but still reliable and protective. "You should name it Maxine," she said.

"The baby? I don't know about that, Mom, and it might be a boy anyway," Ava replied.

"No, not the baby . . . the incubator. You should name it Maxine."

"Agreed." Spencer nodded. "That's perfect."

"Is there some significance to the name?" Graham asked.

"Yes. It was a nurse I met a long time ago. I made a promise to her just before I met Ava's dad. I think she would be very happy right now."

When Ava and Graham told Dr. Davis their news, he asked if they would be willing to document their journey. They agreed with the understanding that their identities would be protected. He then contacted Nicole Darcy, the journalist who had interviewed him over a decade earlier when his conference presentation had made worldwide news. She had kept in contact after the interview and was especially interested in his work because of her traumatic experience with an ectopic pregnancy. He told her she would be the only reporter allowed access, and he also told her she wouldn't be allowed to broadcast any names or faces. Jameson, who'd graduated from college with a degree in filmmaking, would be the videographer. Knowing what an extraordinary opportunity this was, the reporter readily agreed to his terms.

Nicole flew from New York to Tennessee two weeks later to meet with Ava and Graham at their home. Spencer greeted her at the door and took her back to the bedroom where Ava, Graham, Larkin, Aubrey, and Jameson waited with Dr. Davis. Dr. Davis extended his trembling hand to Nicole, and as she took it, she gently steadied it in her grasp. He introduced her to everyone in the group. Ava then showed her their egg, safely housed in the incubator, slowly turning and quickly captivating anyone who witnessed the phenomenon.

"This is truly incredible," Nicole said. "I'll be honest with you all. When I interviewed Dr. Davis, I had my doubts this was even a possibility." She paused and turned to Jameson. "I won't be able to come here as often as I'd like. My producer only knows that I have a project I'm working on that I can't discuss. Thankfully, he trusts me. I appreciate your help. This is an important story that needs to be told. I'll be in frequent communication with you, Ava, and Graham."

"Whatever you need," Jameson replied. "I think today will be a really good start."

Graham removed the egg from the incubator and gently placed it on the bed, cushioned by the thick comforter. He turned on a large camping lantern as Larkin closed the window blinds and Spencer shut the door. Ava anxiously sat on the bed beside the egg while Jameson filmed; Nicole would add the narration later. When the room was dark, Spencer lifted the egg and held the larger end at a slant over the lantern Graham held to illuminate the egg's contents. Larkin quietly prayed that there would not be a blood ring, as she had seen with Susan so many times in the lab.

They were able to see the yolk floating in the middle, anchored on either end by the chalaza (the membrane that attaches the yolk to the shell). In the center of the yolk was the dark spot that would grow into a baby with blood vessels extending from it like delicate red tendrils. Larkin closed her eyes—she was both relieved and overjoyed. As Jameson filmed, Aubrey explained what they were seeing to the future audience. When the brief candling was over, Graham returned the egg to its warm, safe environment.

The group gathered in the living room to discuss the plan for monitoring developmental changes and the growing embryo's health. They'd document everything in detail to help the women and obstetricians who would need guidance in the future. They figured they had about ten more years until other women began laying their own eggs.

Nicole spent the rest of the day with them discussing how this all came to be. They talked about Dr. Davis's mother and his many years of research, Maeve's death, the restrictive changes to abortion and contraception laws, Larkin volunteering, Aubrey's assistance, Ava's first egg, and how all these things had culminated in the life developing in the other room. After many hours of conversation, Nicole returned to New York to begin writing.

As Graham worked nights and Ava worked days, someone would always be home with the egg. Although the incubator had never failed in the lab and they didn't need to be so vigilant, it gave them peace of mind to be there. Spencer wired the incubator with alarms that would ring if the temperature or humidity faltered, and they had a backup generator in case of a power failure.

When their baby had incubated for about eight weeks, Graham and Ava told his parents they were expecting. They would wait until closer to the delivery date to let them know the unconventional way they were expecting. They told his parents they were planning a home delivery, which was very true, but they also told them they would be using a midwife when it would really be Aubrey. His parents questioned Ava and Graham's decision—they couldn't understand delivering the baby outside the safety of a hospital—but the expecting couple decided it was best not to explain anything to them until closer to the delivery.

Ava would wear a false silicone belly throughout the "pregnancy." She started telling her coworkers at the elementary school, and they were joyful about the news. She was due toward the end of April, and she learned Emery was expecting her second child around the same time. Emery's first child was just a few months old, so the other teachers gently teased her about having "Irish twins."

During recess one day, Ava sat on a blue metal bench on the playground as she watched several of her students dangle from the monkey bars and play on the swings. Emery took a seat beside her and congratulated her as she watched her fifth graders play tag.

"Congratulations to you, too, Emery. I hear our due dates are just a few weeks apart."

"Yes. I didn't expect it to happen again so fast, but we're thankful. I think the staff is planning to have a combined baby shower for both of us. Would that be okay with you?"

"Yes, of course. I'm very happy for you."

"Thanks, Ava. I'm happy for you, too. Have you been feeling well? The morning sickness has really hit me hard this time. I've heard that means I'm going to have a girl."

"So far, so good," Ava replied.

"Lucky you! You must be having a boy."

"I've heard that before. Maybe so," Ava replied as she turned away from Emery and focused on the playground.

As they sat side by side watching the children play, Ava blurted out a question. "Hey, Emery . . . I've noticed that a few of the girls in the fifth-grade class have been wearing sunglasses whenever they play outside this year. Do you know why?"

"Well . . . they all have notes from their parents that they have some sort of 'medical condition' making them sensitive to the sun, but, of course, they don't have to tell us legally what that is. But I know. I'm not stupid. I'm sure they're victims of their parents' hysteria and they got involved in that Hen Party cult we heard about when we were teenagers. I feel so sorry for them and what their future holds if it's what I think it is."

Ava turned to ask why she felt sorry for them, but just then, Emery quickly excused herself to go to the restroom—she said she was feeling nauseous.

Alone on the bench, Ava continued watching the girls in their sunglasses playing carefree in the sun. She was happy for them—and excited to not be alone anymore.

CHAPTER 33

During the sixteenth week of incubation, Nicole returned to gather with the family again and check on the egg's progress. Graham and Spencer used a fine drill to cut a small section just large enough for an ultrasound probe into the top of the egg. They had practiced the technique on chicken eggs no fewer than a hundred times to make sure they could do it without harming the egg, leaving the two inner protein membranes intact. They then covered the opening with sterile transparent medical dressing so Aubrey could perform routine monitoring.

"Will doing that help the baby breathe better as well?" Nicole asked as she watched and Jameson recorded. She had returned to witness the first ultrasound and realized how little she knew about how a baby would live and grow within an egg. She had been consumed with writing about how the events of the last several decades had led up to this day but hadn't yet researched how an egg "works."

"The shell is very porous, so air can pass through," Spencer replied. "And the outermost coating, which is called the bloom or cuticle, helps keep bacteria out, so that's why we covered the opening we made with Tegaderm—it prevents germs from entering."

"And the yolk provides all the nourishment?"

"Yes, most of it," Larkin said. "It contains fat, protein, vitamins, and minerals for the growing embryo. When the yolk is completely absorbed, then it's time to hatch."

"And what happens to the egg white?"

"The white portion is the albumen. It's mostly water with some proteins. It also is a source of nourishment and gets absorbed with growth," Larkin said.

"And what if Ava wants to breastfeed the baby?"

"She can use a hormone regimen that induces lactation. Women who adopt infants have successfully breastfed with this method, and Ava would like to do that," Aubrey explained.

Nicole realized she would need to do significant research before completing the documentary. Between Spencer and Larkin's experience with raising chickens and Larkin's years of working with avian embryology, the couple would prove to be a great source of information.

"Well, the heart rate is perfect," Aubrey assured Ava and Graham. "It's steady around 140."

Aubrey kept an external cardiac monitor on the egg to amplify the sound of the heartbeat, the same kind used to monitor chickens, but this was the first time they would be able to see inside the egg. Aubrey had brought her portable ultrasound machine to the house. She connected it to a smart tablet so everyone could see the images on her screen.

"Isn't Dr. Davis joining us?" Nicole asked.

"No, Dad's been slowing down more lately," Jameson said. "He decided to stay home today, but I'll show him what I recorded later. He's incredibly disappointed to be missing this."

Graham placed the egg on the bed for Aubrey.

"Okay . . . if everybody is ready, let's take a look," Aubrey said. She sat on the bed and positioned the transducer on the Tegaderm. As the images appeared on her screen, she said she was astounded by the clarity and thanked Spencer and Graham for their handiwork. She pointed out the fetus's perfect anatomical development and said the measurements were reassuring—they suggested that the incubational age was on target. As she carefully adjusted the egg's angle to get a better look, she asked Ava and Graham if they would like to know their child's sex.

"Whoa! Too late! That's obviously a penis." Larkin laughed as they looked at the screen.

"Yep. No doubt about it. That's my boy!" Graham whooped.

"Congratulations, Ava and Graham. I'm sorry if you wanted to be surprised at birth, but he had other plans." Aubrey smiled.

She would repeat weekly ultrasounds from then until the projected due date for documentation purposes and to make sure their baby boy was developing well. Aubrey explained to Nicole that gestational age is calculated from the date of the last period, but the incubational age would be dated from the time of conception, so a "full term" baby would be thirty-eight weeks and not the traditional forty weeks.

A few weeks later, Nicole returned for another planned ultrasound. This time, Dr. Davis was also there. Jameson helped him into the house, and Ava moved items out of the way so he could navigate toward the bedroom using his walker. His steps were short and shuffling as the tennis balls on the back of the walker glided across the hardwood floors.

"Let's see this baby," he said to Aubrey as he stooped over his walker. His voice was warm.

She showed him the black-and-white images and pointed out the brain, the spine, the kidneys, and the beating heart. He had all of his fingers and toes, and he was sucking his thumb.

"Well, well . . . who would've thunk it?" Dr. Davis said with amazement. Then he chuckled, remembering this phrase as something his father used to say.

"You thunk it, Dad." Jameson laughed from behind the camera.

"Yes, this is your baby, too, Dr. Davis," Ava told him as she held him by the crook of his arm.

Ava's coworkers held the after-school baby shower when Emery was thirty-three weeks pregnant and Ava told them she was thirty weeks along. Ava's false pregnancy belly was getting heavier and more uncomfortable, and she was thankful she was able to remove it when she got home. She couldn't imagine how Emery was feeling. The other teachers commented that Ava was "all belly." They remarked that she didn't seem to gain weight anywhere else, and her feet were amazingly unswollen. Ava mumbled that she guessed she was just lucky and gave credit to her mother's genetics.

Half of the teachers' lounge was decorated with blue balloons and the other half with pink for Emery's baby—her prediction had been correct about having a girl. Gift bags with drawings of sheep and clouds and elephants covered one table, and another table had a punch bowl and cupcakes topped with ducklings and pacifiers. There were also multiple jars of unlabeled baby food to use in a game later. A calendar hung on the wall for everyone to guess the delivery dates.

Ava was thanking her friends for organizing the shower when she realized Emery wasn't there. One of the fifth-grade teachers said Emery had gone to see her obstetrician that morning because she had a headache and felt dizzy. They hadn't heard an update yet, but Emery had asked them to start without her if she wasn't back on time.

As the group taste-tested the pureed mystery foods, trying to guess which ones were squash and peas and green beans, the principal came in to let them know Emery's husband had called. She'd had an emergency C-section due to severe preeclampsia. The baby was in the NICU because she had some fluid in her lungs but was expected to be fine in a day or two. Even so, the baby might have to stay a little longer in the NICU to make sure she was feeding well and maintaining her body temperature—a common issue for premature babies. She was expected to be home in about a week.

The teachers murmured prayers and support, and they all texted words of encouragement to Emery. Some warned Ava that preeclampsia was more common with first babies; they hoped she had a good obstetrician who was monitoring her urine and blood pressure for any signs that she might be getting ill. Ava reassured them she was being checked closely and her baby was doing well.

She texted love and support to Emery before loading a generous number of gifts into her car. Then she went home to take off the prosthetic and check on her baby.

It was only two more weeks until their baby boy would be full term, so Graham and Ava invited his parents to the house so they could talk.

When they arrived, Ava was wearing a T-shirt and jeans, clearly not pregnant. Graham told them Ava wasn't pregnant, but they were having a baby. His parents thought he was telling them a bizarre joke—his dad told him to be serious as they were not amused. Graham's mom looked at Ava quizzically and asked if they had decided to use a surrogate but hadn't mentioned it for some reason. "Can you not carry a baby yourself?" she asked Ava.

Ava looked to Graham to explain.

"No, Mom. There is no surrogate," Graham assured them.

Ava and Graham brought his parents to their bedroom and showed them the incubator where their future grandchild was being housed. Graham's parents stared in silence for a few moments before they began berating Graham and Ava.

"This is absolutely absurd," his father said angrily. "What have the two of you done? You two have been part of that crazy Hen Party bullshit we heard about ten years ago? You've been hiding this from us the whole time?"

"You married her knowing this—*this*—is how you would have a baby? Or did she not tell you until after she had the ring on her finger?" his mother said, looking at Ava with disdain.

"What in the holy hell?" his dad said. "Will it be normal? Is it going to have feathers or something? Jesus Christ, Graham. What were you thinking? Were either of you even thinking?" Enraged, he threw his hands in the air.

Graham's mother started pacing the floor and muttering. "Oh my God, oh my God, oh my God. I can't believe this. We were so excited for this grandbaby." Then she started crying.

"And Spencer and Larkin had to know all this, right? So they have been in on this deception as well, haven't they?" Graham's father bellowed at Ava.

"So," Graham said calmly. "*It* is a boy, and, yes, *he* will be normal. He will not have feathers or a beak or a comb on his head. He will look like any other baby boy. Same end result as any other pregnancy, just different packaging."

"And, yes, my parents knew," Ava added. "We're keeping this as private as we can, but we would like you to both be here when he's born."

Graham urged his parents to sit on the couch in the den. Once they were settled, he handed them ultrasound pictures.

"See? He is just like any other baby."

They held the photos and looked at the images of their future grandson. His mother looked at Ava with tears in her eyes.

"You know," his mom started to explain. "I had a horrible pregnancy with Graham. I was on bed rest from twenty-two weeks until his delivery because I had an incompetent cervix. *Incompetent*—what a horrible thing to tell a frightened young mother." She shook her head in disbelief as she recalled the doctor's words. "Telling me that my body was inadequate, not good enough. It was a scary and awful experience. I was only able to keep him inside me until he was almost twenty-nine weeks old. He was unbelievably tiny." She traced the outline of her grandbaby on the ultrasound photo as she spoke.

"He was in the neonatal intensive care unit for almost six weeks," Graham's father added. "Had to have a tube down into his lungs so they could give him medicine to make his lungs stronger and he could breathe." He patted his wife's hand.

"We could only be with him at certain times of the day," his mother said, looking at Ava. "It was torture not to be able to hold him. Then his dad caught the RSV infection and couldn't visit Graham for a while because it could have killed him." She paused at the awful memory. "When we finally got to take him home, we were relieved, but I sunk into a deep postpartum depression because I blamed myself for all of it. Me and my 'incompetent' cervix." She emphasized that horrible word with contempt. "It took me a long time not to blame myself. It was just the anatomy I was given." She waved her hands dismissively.

"That does sound just awful," Ava said sympathetically.

"Yes, it was. You know? It would have been much easier on both of us to have had Graham grown in an egg instead," his mother mused. After a moment, she continued. "But . . . he grew into this really strong, smart, handsome guy with a beautiful and equally wonderful wife." Graham's father nodded in agreement.

"We really want you to be with us for the delivery," Graham said sincerely.

"We'll be there."

CHAPTER 34

We have not wings, we cannot soar;
But we have feet to scale and climb
By slow degrees, by more and more,
The cloudy summits of our time.
—Henry Wadsworth Longfellow

Once Aubrey confirmed that the yolk had completely absorbed, it was time for the . . . delivery? The hatching? The birth? They were unsure of what to call it, but it didn't matter. They were all there gathered in Graham and Ava's home, all except for Dr. Davis. Graham and Ava, of course, but also all the others who had participated in this evolving adventure—Aubrey, Spencer, Larkin, Graham's parents, Nicole, and Jameson. Susan happily accepted an invitation to attend as well.

After developing pneumonia, Dr. Davis had been admitted to the hospital a week earlier. Jameson, Aubrey, and Larkin had visited him daily. He was weak but talkative, wanting updates on the baby. He had been moved to the ICU the day before because he needed closer observation and had to have fluid removed from his lungs. They promised to bring him Jameson's recording.

Graham and Ava's bed was covered with a plush white blanket that Graham's parents had brought as one of many baby gifts. Laid next to the blanket were ample supplies for neonatal resuscitation that Aubrey had brought, if needed. She had completed her recertification a few months earlier.

Spencer had wanted the new parents to have a fancy tool to open the egg, one that was suitable for the occasion, so he'd soldered a blunt tip to the head of a small hammer and then spray-painted it gold. He bowed toward Graham and presented it to him with a flourish. Graham then bowed down to accept it. He laid it on the bed and walked to the incubator. When Graham turned off the incubator, the room went silent. He removed the egg for the last time and laid it on the bed. Ava sat on the bed as the others gathered around. Jameson stood and filmed, focused only on the egg.

Graham held the modified hammer over the egg, in the spot where the air sac was located, and asked, "Okay . . . are we ready?"

No one said anything. They were all frozen with anticipation.

"I'd say that's a yes," he said, then took a deep breath as Ava held the egg steady.

Tap-tap-tap.

"Easy now . . . easy," Spencer urged.

"Yes, yes. I know. I'm being easy."

Tap-tap.

"Can you see his hair? What color is it?" Graham's mother interrupted.

He sighed and continued.

Tap-tap-tap-tap-tap-tap.

"Still nothing?" his dad asked.

"Please, just let us focus, okay?" Graham urged.

Tap-tap-tap-tap.

CRACK.

Ava gasped.

"That's it! Peel off the rest of it!" Larkin said excitedly.

"So, is his hair brown?" Graham's mother asked again.

"Please, Mom . . . give us a sec, okay?"

Pieces of glistening shell dropped to the floor, revealing remnants of amnion coating a head of thick, brown hair. Gently, after Graham had removed the rest of the shell to expose his ruddy, smooth skin, Graham and Ava dried off their new baby boy, Efron.

Efron started crying immediately—a strong first wail followed by several softer and shorter bleats that sounded like a baby goat.

Graham's parents folded the blanket that contained the shell and put it in a nearby chair so Ava could sit up in the bed to hold him.

Larkin placed him on Ava's chest, and Ava offered her breast to soothe him. He latched on immediately and suckled. The induced lactation regimen had worked.

As Efron nursed, Ava inspected every little feature of her baby.

"He has a belly button!" Ava exclaimed.

"Yes," Larkin confirmed. "And see? He has a little bit of umbilical cord from where it was attached to the yolk. He's just like other babies. Well, of course, I think he's above average since he's my grandson."

When Efron dozed off after his first feeding, Ava swaddled him tightly. Then everyone took turns holding him and agreeing on how perfect he was. Larkin was overcome with emotion as she gazed at a life that less than an hour ago had been encased in a shell. She was so thankful. Thankful for Dr. Davis's mother, whose untimely death had inspired her son. Thankful for Dr. Davis's brilliant mind. Thankful for her husband and the friends who had supported her. Thankful for the daughter who understood her.

And it made Larkin think of Maeve and how she felt she'd failed her so long ago. That pain, that anguish would always be with her, but seeing her grandson in her daughter's arms gave her comfort and hope.

When Jameson was done filming, Nicole thanked the family profusely for giving her the opportunity to be both an eyewitness and a reporter. She hoped to complete her work within a few months and then broadcast it to the world. It was unbelievable, and it was going to be quite a story to tell.

Jameson packed up his recording equipment and told Larkin he would call after visiting his dad in the ICU and playing him the video of Efron's birth. Her phone rang a few hours later. "Hi, Jameson! So, how is he doing? What did he think?" Larkin asked.

"Larkin . . . Dad died. The pneumonia worsened. He knew he wasn't going to survive this, but he wasn't scared. He said he was fulfilled. He didn't get to see the recording of Efron, but I told him everything. He was so pleased."

"I'm so very sorry, Jameson."

"He made me promise to tell you something he said was important, Larkin. He said to look for him in his next incarnation."

"Did he say what he might be?"

"Yes—a duck."

ACKNOWLEDGMENTS

To my brother, Ron and my sister-in-law, Nikki, for their endless patience and support. To my husband, Mike, for being my most enthusiastic fan with unwavering positivity. To my best friend, Kathryn, for always lifting my spirits when I would spiral into self-doubt.

Much appreciation to my parents for instilling in me a love of reading and encouraging me to make my voice be heard. And thanks to my brother, Richard, for reinforcing their teachings.

Thank you, Dr. Robert Minkoff, for giving me my first job as a research scientist and making me into a bona fide "chickenologist" before I became a medical doctor.

For reading and commenting on the early iterations of my manuscript, I thank my friends: Suzanne Schierholt Smith, Joy Bisesi, and Aubrey King. I also thank the professionals who helped me with invaluable input: Megann Kammerman, Amy Vrana, and Lindsey Salatka.

My website would not exist without the generous help and incredible talent of Larken Lech.

Thank you to Brooke Warner and the She Writes Press team for your enthusiasm, hard work, and this amazing opportunity. Thank you to the publicity and marketing team at Books Forward for your support and our shared love of puns.

This book would not have been written without the US Supreme Court decision of June 24, 2022, so I reluctantly thank six of the justices for their inspiration. A sincere thank you to Justices Breyer, Sotomayor and Kagan for their dissent. And thank you Justice Jackson for sharing the poem that has been your guiding principle.

Finally, thank you to my own little bird, Ava. I'm looking forward to hearing your stories. Always remember that life has just one period but many, many commas.

ABOUT THE AUTHOR

Author photo © Nancy Labib

Victoria Dillon is a former research scientist, current pediatrician and writer with a passion for exploring the intersections of politics and science. She has a unique ability to blend speculative fiction with thought-provoking social commentary, creating prose that speaks both to the heart and the mind. She has lived in the South throughout her childhood and career and loves naps with her cat, Americana music, and hunting for her next read at Parnassus Books in Nashville, Tennessee. She currently resides in Middle Tennessee.

Looking for your next great read?

We can help!

Visit www.shewritespress.com/next-read or scan the QR code below for a list of our recommended titles.

She Writes Press is an award-winning independent publishing company founded to serve women writers everywhere.